Chronicles

of

Two

Wolves

RABBIT HOUSE PRESS
Versailles, KY 40383

Published in the United States of America by Rabbit House Press, September 2023.

For inquiries about author appearances and/or volume orders contact us at rabbithousepress.com.

ISBN: 979-8-9871928-6-3

Editor: Vickie Elkins
Cover and interior design; formatting: Brooke Lee

Chronicles

of

Two

Wolves

A Path to Heart Spirit

Palmer E. Tolly & James Riordan

RABBIT
HOUSE
PRESS
rabbithousepress.com

Robert Mullinax
Portrait of Rick Two Wolves, 2023
Acrylic wash

Mullinax was a featured artist in *Modern Mountain Magazine* and won Best Debut Artist at the Native American Music Awards in 2014 as a Native flute performer.

ACKNOWLEDGMENTS

I had a hunch that this would be a difficult subject for me. As I acknowledge all the beings and energies that have been before me, beside me and behind me, I feel a flood of humility.

This book exists because of the insight and encouragement from the world-renowned and remarkable author and very dear friend, James Riordan. Your vision inspired me to embrace strengths, transforming the topography of my creative world. Your alchemy of word usage is a noble gift. As I visited the corridors of alternate dimensions, you encouraged me to put into print a unique reality, a legacy of profound purpose. Thank you for inviting me to write this book and especially for believing in me.

I thank my son Rick Two Wolves for bringing into my journey an unexpected opportunity and experience in both the maternal and the spiritual realm. Together, we found paths and energetic networks I would not have dreamed I would encounter. I never gave up on you, and you never gave up on me. I am proud to be your mother.

Calvin, a spiritual teacher to the world through example of endurance and preservation, has proven himself an exceptional warrior. You behold the ability achieving through your own merit a higher consciousness, proving yourself to be an extraordinary teacher by example.

To all my family who welcomed Rick into their life I give thanks. Paul Tolly, my husband of thirty years, selflessly volunteered to embrace Rick, allowing him for the first time, to have a Dad who was accepting, fair and loving.

To Ambie Tolly, who was both an official in the Department of Family Services and also a big sister to Rick, I hope you know how much it meant for you to be there for support and hold my hand when needed.

Thank you to Billie Bradford, a sister who *always* remembers Rick's special days. You are the best aunt on earth.

To Helga Condon, you are, indeed, a friend extraordinaire. Thanks for reaching out to Rick.

My friend and colleague, Renee Williams, Licensed Clinical Professional Counselor, who as a best friend and confidant, would hold me up through the most difficult days while also providing exceptional professional support to both Rick Two Wolves and his brother Calvin in their adolescent years. I miss you always!

To the nurturing and loving woman, Donna, who opened her heart and home to Calvin—always offering love and acceptance to the brothers without reserve. You became my sister.

Joseph Many Horses Davis, thank you for reviewing this manuscript. Your diligence rendered both guidance and good counsel to share the indigenous ways with respect and honor.

The Native American Community of the Two Feathers Medicine Clan: To Chief Joseph Big Feather Schallmo, Richard Pony Soldier Byrd and family, Cynthia Crow Woman Staples and Joseph Many Horses Davis. Your spirit medicine is powerful–for which I give thanks.

The completion of this book in 2022 was not without the endless reassurance from my life partner, Paul M. Osborne. When I forgot to eat while working on the book, he served me fresh coffee and snacks. It didn't matter if it was a computer tech problem or if I needed a sketch for a graphic concept, he would deliver. He always said "yes"!

William E. Bradford, former writer for Associated Press and author and brother–in–law, a man generous with his skills, encouraging and previewing the manuscript. Your observations and comments were spot on.

Jo Ellen Wilhoite, Copy Editor and friend, your diligence in reviewing manuscripts showered me with inspiration. Much love and appreciation.

Robert Mullinax, so very gifted as both an artist and a musician, thank you. You embody the very essence of the grace and honesty of Mother Earth.

There are many unsung heroes who not only reach out to Rick Two Wolves, but to many others in need of support and encouragement. To Will Carson from the Outreach program at Thresholds, always remember that you make a difference. Thank you.

To all who have given service on this journey, both in the earth plane and the heavens—I thank you for your assistance. I may not have known how or why you helped, but that's okay with me. Accept these words as my nod of utmost respect. Please bless this book and guide it to its highest purpose.

Thank you,

Palmer

CONTENTS

INTRODUCTION

The term Heart Spirit first began as a whimsical curiosity. Does the human heart have its own spirit? This was the question that looped in my thoughts like an intriguing puzzle. From a metaphysical framework, the idea that the heart must be more than a pump, a mere physical organ, felt legitimate. The intuitive hunch was only the beginning. Insatiable research into areas that included Chinese Traditional Medicine, writings of sage authors and wisdom of many mentors opened a doorway to new knowledge and inspiration that would never be closed.

Chronicles of Two Wolves: A Path to Heart Spirit is a summation of personal life experiences, the imagination and spiritual vision. It courses from bottomless pits to heights of miracles, giving hope and healing to children seeking help and refuge in a cruel world. Meticulous documentation is presented to give both credibility and authority to the material presented. However, the story also navigates in and out of metaphoric and mythical design: symbolism to touch many levels of awareness, both conscious and unconscious, in the reader.

The philosopher and American writer, Joseph Campbell teaches: "Mythology is a production of the Wisdom body, not the intellect…Myths have come from the vision world…The journey of the hero is about the courage to seek the depths; the image of creative rebirth; the eternal cycle of change within us; the uncanny discovery that the seeker is the mystery which the seeker seeks to know."

The Chronicles of Two Wolves not only illustrates many of the insights of Campbell's *The Hero's Journey*, it also proves beyond a doubt that truth is stranger than fiction. These truths and events reverberate far beyond the authors. And, if we can be a humble messenger, challenge accepted. We took the risks. For the unsung heroes everywhere, for the two boys from Paragould, Arkansas—the risks must be taken. Staying on the straight path certainly achieved results but jumping into the unknown harbored exciting new possibilities that needed to be explored. Identifying and following, no, embracing the right path was one thing. But, ensuing that path through experiences of young warriors whose primary qualification was the resolute courage to go on, is quite something else. This was the higher purpose, a subjective one to be sure, nevertheless, of great value for those who are meant to receive it. It is our sincere hope that we achieved it for you.

Palmer Tolly & James Riordan

Chapter One

THE ASTRAL CONVERGENCE

Then towards the end of the Ceremony, I kept hearing the phrase repeating louder and louder, "We are many, we are strong"–the spirits departed. It was as if a very ancient agreement had been awakened at the appointed time...
~ Thomas Pecora[1]

The horizon was infinite, extending beyond what any normal human eye could see. An expansive sun in the distance gave off a rosy golden glow. An orb resembling Saturn, adorned with rings, was definitely not in its orbital place. Planetary objects were not in the usual expected order, certainly not conforming to the logistics of an earth perspective. It appeared to be daytime, yet heavenly bodies only seen in the night sky were conspicuously visible. That this was an astral plane was the most probable explanation, a world of pure idea adhering to basic laws of the universe, the consciousness of the highest form of energy.

The foliage was thick, the soil velvet black. It would seem that plants had been blooming perennially over eons. Perhaps the planetary rotation generated atypical cycles, at least compared to Earth's patterns. There was, however, the recognizable earthly beauty of a steep waterfall, mammoth vegetation, and the warmth of familial fauna emitting an aura of harmony and tranquility. An assembly of the spirit persuasion, clad in mantles of ancient times, formed a broad circle. Wisdom Keepers from many ancient tribes, animal totems, healers, mystics, spirits from the angelic realm, and a few curious hitch-hiking faery folk, gathered for the occasion. All entities present were there to fulfill a plan designed to help earthlings of future generations better understand their energies for the purpose of healing themselves, other beings and the planet. In this sacred gathering, the past, present, and future cosmically melded into oneness.

DIGNITARIES IN ATTENDANCE

Chief Duke Joseph Big Feather Schallmo, a six foot tall stocky individual, stood poised as a prominent figure. In the future 1900's, he will become the designated spiritual leader of an intertribal group called Two Feathers Medicine Clan. Although officially formed in the early 1800's, their original work and traditions precede that date by centuries. The Chief was volunteering to be of service to many earthlings struggling with injustice and abuse. He will assist in the life journey of a youth yet to be born in the year 1980.

Horn Chips will begin one of his incarnations on earth year 1836. He was identified as an honored invitee. The future history will reveal that he was orphaned when he was a young child, to be raised by his grandmother.[2] He and Crazy Horse were childhood friends. Crazy Horse, born in the Black Hills of South Dakota in 1841, was the son of the Oglala Sioux shaman, also named Crazy Horse, and his wife, a member of the Brule Sioux. It is written that Horn Chips was adopted by the uncle of Crazy Horse. The relationship between Horn Chips and Crazy Horse became stronger after Horn Chips, as Medicine Man, made a war medicine for Crazy Horse. Crazy Horse will be Chief, mystic and warrior for his people. Old man Horn Chips will beget two sons, Ellis Chips and Joe Chips. Ellis Chips and his wife Victoria had three sons, Charles, Phillip, and Godfrey.

Horn Chips was in attendance at this Astral Convergence to arrange the future encounter of his grandson, Godfrey, with a young Cherokee man in the year of 1996. Godfrey would be known in future generations to have strong medicine for the Cherokee male youth.

Among the gathered was a humble Cherokee man who would arrive on earth on August 17th, 1935. Richard Pony Soldier Byrd will officiate sacred ceremonies and provide sage guidance to the Two Feathers Medicine Clan. The urban ceremonial leader will oversee a naming ceremony for a male yet to be born year of 1980. And so, it was to be.

The summit began with the voice of Zitkála-Šá,[3] earth life, 1876–1938. As a writer, composer, lecturer, and activist, she was known as one of the first and foremost American Indian reformers. Extraordinarily gifted on the violin, Zitkála-Šá's performances for the president and abroad, notably in Paris, brought her international acclaim. Musical passion compelled her to create a fusion of classical music with her native culture, which resulted in her composing the Sundance Opera. Zitkála-Šá devoted her life to sharing her culture through major publications. She created children's stories and fought for Native American justice. Stepping into the circle she addressed the members with strength and clarity, "In my early childhood, I was free as the wind and no less spirited than an abounding deer…I remember the day I lost my spirit. It was not when we reached the school grounds. It was not when my native clothes were taken away and replaced with a dress that scratched my skin-and hard shoes that pinched my feet. It was the next morning when I heard talk about cutting my long heavy hair. I did my best to hide, but I was found. Strong hands carried me fast and tied me to a chair. I cried and shook my head wildly till I felt the cold blades of the scissors against my neck. Then my keepers gnawed off my thick braids and cut my hair in a shingles style that labeled me a coward. I lost my spirit that day. I could not know that it would rise again, stronger, wiser for the winds that it had suffered."

Giving herself the name Zitkála-Šá (*Red Bird*), she would bear witness to the power of calling back her spirit through the ceremony of "naming" in the native way. "There will be the calling back of one's spirit for many who walk the earth path," voiced Chief Joseph Big Feather Schallmo. Foreshadowing the future when he returns to earth, he exclaimed, "We are here to bring the light to the hearts of our ancestors of the future."

The leader and moderator of this convention was the elder Medicine Woman, Miko. Her name translated into the English word for *chief.* She was from the Choctaw Nation, a descendant of the Hopewell and Mississippian cultures,who lived throughout the east of the Mississippi River valley 1,700 years ago. Her skirt, made of buckskin, fell loosely to her ankles, augmented by a mantle of turkey feathers. Miko's silver hair was neatly pulled back into a single braid. A beaded necklace, imaging the diamonds on the respected rattlesnake, hung gracefully upon her breast. Choctaw ancestors highly regard the rattlesnake because of its powerful venom and dominance among other creatures. Miko was known for her own powerful medicine. She was deemed an esteemed ancestor of past, present, and future.

Miko began, "Sharing fireside talks, songs, ceremonies with relatives, the elements of wind, fire, water, and the earth helps us to remember our connection to the Great Mystery. This gathering shall be part of our shared oral stories into the future." She then addressed two wolves, or wayas, known by the names Shadow Dancer and Egahi, sitting attentively near her feet. "My esteemed emissaries, you will walk upon the earth in search of a sacred portal, Sipapu, the sacred door to Heart Spirit. Along your journey there will be guides and guardians to assist you. You must see the unseen messages in the leaves, look into each droplet of rain, bubbles on the surface of the streams and the invisible breath of the winds. When the thunder beings speak, listen. Most of all, heed the great mystery of lightning. It mirrors the spirit of the universe." She raised her arm with a finger pointing to the sky, adding, "remember that the universe is a fractal. Whatever energy signature we carry will be repeated infinitely, again and again…until we change that vibration."

Although made up of many different indigenous and cultural tribes, the assembly said the Lakota prayer in unison, "Aho Mitakuye oyasin." This translates to "we are all related" or "all of my relations." This includes not only family but friends, nature, rocks, bugs, etc.; a very common and often used ending. It's like Amen at the end of something important. The "aho" that frequently precedes is merely a casual acknowledgment of that phrase.

Chapter Two

EARTH PLANE

Keep close to nature's heart…break clear away once in a while. Climb a mountain or spend a week in the woods. Wash your spirit clean.
~ John Muir

The wayas, wolves, held firm their stride on a barely visible path covered in the layers of pine needles and dead leaves of many seasons past. The atmosphere held rustic smells of old trees while exposing a plethora of the sweet scents of new growth. It was rare to find an earthly space so unspoiled by the human footprint. This remote wilderness, known as the Boreal Forest, was home to numerous species of mammals, shrubs, conifers, flora, and fauna. Migratory birds, waterfowl, songbirds, and raptors, numbered in the millions, emerged seasonally, soaring into the world beyond.

The pair of traveling wolves came from the Wolf Clan, commonly referred to as Waya Clan. The male, sporting a deep ebony coat, was appropriately named Shadow Dancer. The female waya, donning a white coat reminiscent of the wild arctic tundra, was known as Egahi, Cherokee for *light*. The rhythm of their paws sounded on the ground in a steady pace, akin to a soft drumbeat. There could be no question that the two were energetically synchronized as one. As the tired sun crept below the horizon, they morphed into silhouettes against the darkening amber sky.

The wayas were from the Grey Wolf species, which were known to wear the fur of many different colors. Originally from different packs or tribes, they had been summoned from the ancestral realms. Bequeathed the same sacred quest, the two wayas bonded immediately as if they had been raised in the same pack.

The long journey may have discouraged other wolves, but their keen instincts led them to believe that this mission was about much more than time or distance. After all, the pair held the auspicious title of Gamma wolves. This honor was reserved for the elders of the pack greatly respected for their powerful medicine. Their legendary reputation for storytelling had been passed from generation to generation. The importance of the expedition was met with unflinching determination and a sense of privilege. Divine providence had sent them to fulfill the prophecy of Sipapu. It was their destiny to discover an elusive portal, an opening to the spirit that lives within the heart.

A golden mist appeared from the refraction of the sun's rays, filling the atmosphere. If the wayas could have been captured on canvas by the impressionist, Monet, the creatures would have dissolved into the milieu, both concealing and revealing their oneness with nature.

Chapter Three

COMPLIMENTARIES

The most dangerous psychological mistake is the projection of the shadow on to others: this is the root of almost all conflicts.
~ Carl Jung

"I rather enjoy our twilight treks," said Shadow Dancer to his loyal companion.

"The dwindling of daylight welcomes the arrival of campfires of the spirits in the heavens," Egahi replied. "Night is soon upon us."

"It is my nature to be elusive," Shadow Dancer proclaimed. "I am Shadow Dancer. I appear under the moonbeams and the stars in the night firmament." He adds in a humble tone. "I am pleasured that you find such favor in my presence. However, many of my students do not. The lesson to look at the shadow side is not welcomed."

"Remember that such ill sentiments of which you speak mirror the many fears and wounds yet to heal," Egahi said defensively."It is often difficult to face our shortcomings and weaknesses. Someday, when there is sufficient courage for your students to understand, truth will be revealed. Until then, your messages remain uncelebrated."

"I am the most unpopular Gamma for sure," Shadow Dancer sighed.

"But I cannot undertake this mission alone," Egahi impatiently responded. "Together we are balance. A shadow is only as visible as the brightness of the light. We both exist as principles of complementaries. Yin & Yang symbols describe something very elemental and incredibly complex. We are light and shadow, together we are whole."

"In the oral tradition, there is a story that the Moon, Kanati', the Great Hunter, had fallen in love with a Star Maiden, the Sun, chasing her across the sky. The beautiful Star Maiden was never where he looked. To make matters worse, Kanati' was hopelessly lost in finding a home, a space where they could be together as one. Kanati', quite the romantic, relentlessly crossed a heavenly orbit, day after night, day after night, in pursuit of his Star Maiden. Then, behold! Upon the day of the Lunar Eclipse, Kanati', the moon, and his love, the Sun, find that space and time in the cosmos to be together as one. Let the Moon chasing the Sun be a reminder that the shadow must seek the light. The shadow lives only when light lives," said Egahi as they sauntered along.

Egahi slowed her pace, suggesting a pause. Resting from the journey, Egahi lay down belly up, playfully flitting leaves dangling on a low hanging limb of the oak species. With growing fascination, she realized that each tree branch, from the trunk to the tips mirrored the limb from which it had sprouted. From mother branch to daughter branch, an exact, yet smaller version had developed. Inquisitively, Shadow Dancer scrutinized Egahi's discovery wondering if this self-similarity is merely an anomaly or rather a phenomenon omnipresent in nature.

A patch of lycophytes, plants that dated from the Silurian (425 million years ago), seized Shadow Dancer's attention. One of the oldest of vascular plants, Lycophytes, are believed to be the living lineage of vascular plants, evolved during the Silurian Period. A common name for this family is Wolf Foot. It had been observed that roots and branch tips resembled a wolf's paw. It was an earnest reminder to the wayas that although they exist in the present realm, the connection of pre-civilization also co-existed in like manner.

Finding themselves amid dense clusters of lush ferns, Egahi speaks, "The indigenous Maori of New Zealand holds true that the fern represents new life and new beginnings. To our Asian neighbors, it symbolizes family and the hope for future generations."

Investigating each leaf vein with curiosity, they were hopeful to learn more clues from nature's database. The fronds of a nearby fern split and divided into leaflets, and those into sub-leaflets, revealing the eternal pattern built into the plant's dominion. The observation of self-similar patterns seemed to be popping up everywhere around them. The echoes of Miko's words floated through their minds, "Whatever energy signature we carry will be repeated infinitely, again and again…"

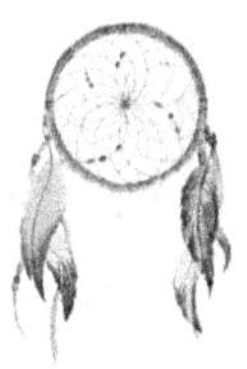

Chapter Four

THE NEW KID

The littlest feet make the biggest footprint in our hearts.

~ Author unknown

March 1980, at 11:56 o'clock earth years, the infant, Ricky Wayne Davis, Jr., was born into this world. His birth was to Mary Jane and Rick Wayne Davis on Friday, the 7th at the Community Methodist Hospital. His weight at birth was six pounds and nine ounces and he was nineteen and a half inches long. The family lived in Paragould, Arkansas, found in the southeast of the center of Greene County, nine miles east of the Missouri state line at the St.

Francis River. Ricky Davis' heritage was Cherokee and mixed European ancestry. On this March Day, the dark-eyed infant drew his first breath, then exhaled, signaling to the cosmos "I'm the new kid". His arrival would not be of much notice to the world. Yet, it is believed that many forces, seen and unseen, were attentive to such matters. Like dancing jugglers in the cosmos, a celestial plan was in motion. The obvious obscurity and apparent inconsequential event of Ricky Davis' birth would not elude certain energetic paths, as foretold by Miko at the Astral Convergence.

By the time Ricky was six, he had three younger siblings, Brian Michael, William Jay, who was called B.J., and the baby, Elizabeth. His Grandmother, Gladys Davis, in sharing early history, spoke of her son's wife. Mary Jane, the children's mother, had a history of drug usage and occasional disappearances. Gladys' son and Ricky's father, Rick Sr. would often leave to search for her, leaving the four little ones on their own. But they were not completely on their own, for young Ricky, even at age six, would take on the task of caring for his siblings. It must be noted that, Ricky, as the eldest of the pack, must have had strong wolf medicine, i.e., strong family loyalty. He would lovingly attempt to feed his brothers and diaper his baby sister, Elizabeth, who was about one at the time. Ricky was operating on pure love and instinct. He did his best.

Eventually, Gladys and Robert Davis, the paternal grandparents, realized that they needed to take action. After pursuing blood tests to ascertain that the children were indeed her son's progeny, Gladys pursued legal action to adopt the four children. Neither parent stepped forward to prevent the legal process. The life of family with Grandma and Grandpa Davis began, which would be for Ricky, the most treasured and precious memories of his early childhood.

Ricky held a deep affection for his family, displaying acts of kindness by caring for his siblings and donning the role of a big brother, or perhaps, the leader of the pack. Now living with Grandma and Grandpa, family was becoming more important with each day for Ricky. He entered kindergarten at the age of five, attending Oak Grove Elementary School in Paragould.

Ricky enjoyed sharing stories about his active life in the creek running along the side of their home.

I'd play in the nearby creek catchin' crawdads—sometimes with my little sis. We were doing everything we could possible to get dirty as hell. Yeah, if you aren't caked in dirt, you didn't have a good day! I didn't keep em'—I'd put them back in the creek. What games did we play? Well, if you wanna count redneck games, everything was done either around a swing set or an old-fashioned tire swing.

When swept up in joy and elation, Ricky could send out a beautiful howl like a wolf. Spontaneous and in the moment, it was a bit comical when observed, yet his intent was pure emotion. Young Ricky was free spirited, hyperactive, disarmingly friendly, and especially lovable. Terms like warrior, unstoppable, resourceful, and ingenious all accurately describe the young Ricky in his early years, but clearly his spirit was most defined by his love for his family. The adoption by Gladys and Bob Davis provided a family system that well supported the basic needs of the little boy and his siblings. Although their mother, Mary Jane, had sporadic visits, according to Grandma, it tended to add turmoil and confusion for the young Davis children. In spite of this, their lives grew into normal lives with cousins and friends.

Despite an occasional old-fashioned Arkansas switching when he misbehaved, Ricky was happy hunting for crawdads in the nearby creek with his little brothers and feasting on Sunday breakfast of grandma's famous homemade biscuits. Rick's identity was starting to form nicely. He knew who he was: Ricky Wayne Davis Jr., a Davis who lived with the Davis family. He thrived and his spirit flourished.

It is said by elders, to look into the eyes of a child is to see their soul, and in seeing the soul, it is possible to see into the heart, the heart and spirit as one. The Cherokee use the same word for both heart and spirit, a d nv do, (oo-da-na-doe).

RICKY'S JOURNAL 4/24/93

When I was living with my grandparents, I had lots of fun. They had a nice black dog named Lady. I had a little sister named Elizabeth. She always called my grandma and grandpa, mommy and daddy.

Life was busy and hectic. Gladys and Bob Davis, having raised three boys and a daughter to adulthood, felt overwhelmed. So, when Gladys met Robert and Diana Benson while playing bingo and learned that they were childless, an idea was born which was destined to dramatically change many lives, especially that of little Ricky and his younger brother, Brian.

Chapter Five

A RAVEN NAMED JESSE

The raven is a significant figure in most Native American cultures. It is seen as the creator of light and as a trickster figure.

Many of the old trees had fallen, hinting Mother Nature had been a bit slack with her housekeeping. The recent storms had scrambled things up a touch. Scraps of branches from a large sycamore heaped upon the path. Shadow Dancer and Egahi took caution stepping in a slower stride. Their trek was growing more capricious as they navigated around a carpet of tangled brambles. In spite of their cunning as Gamma wolves, they began to harbor doubts of their prowess as hunters of *Sipapu*.

Turbulence in the air was accompanied by the sounds of flapping wings. A large raven, known by the name "Jesse," swooped down landing on a rock pile covered with layers of dead leaves. The trio seemed pleased to see one another. Their paths had crossed before and always under favorable circumstances.

The relationship between wolves and ravens was not just symbiotic, but also playful. Sometimes the wolves would respond to a raven's call heralding a great find—food, which gave ample feast to each and all. Wolves were commonly known to follow ravens when sighted nearby. With instincts maximized from their pleasant reunion, it was understood that the raven would help them find an alternate path to their destination. As the bird lifted off into the light of the Green Corn Moon, De ha luyi, Shadow Dancer and Egahi followed. Jesse led them into an enchanting landscape, a region densely blanketed with flora of eerie splendor. The wayas' eyes dilated at the sights and sounds of a whippoorwill near a glistening stream. An opportunity to rest at the mouth of a cavern was not missed.

Their eyes wondered into the night sky. The glint of a shooting star darting above seemed to leap about for their mere pleasure. In the southern hemisphere during summer months, astrological designs in the celestial arena were typically visible from earth. One constellation, however, radiated with exceptional brightness—Orion.

The well-known astrological formation held great stature in indigenous cultures. There was, however, a unique and profound connection between the Hopi people and the Orion constellation. The Hopi are believed to have settled in a location they considered to be the center of the universe. When connected to other Hopi monuments and landmarks around the Southwest, the collective group forms a map of the entire constellation of Orion. The celestial pattern, familiar to the wayas, was perceptible from deep inside the cave as well. Bioluminescent worm colonies, mimicking the night sky, hung from the ceiling in hammocks of their own silk. Delicate threads hung down like Mardi Gras beads. Naive moths were tricked by the dangling sticky strings that shimmered like crystal chandeliers.[4] A clear and distinct re-creation of the constellation *Orion* punctuated the otherwise blackness in the cave. The masquerade of the night sky was indeed an effective decoy. The hosts would feast well tonight.

As the trio retreated, Jesse flew into the opening, leading Egahi and Shadow Dancer towards a peculiar symbol. A shallow carving into the outer cave was that of a Hopi kiva. In the Hopi tradition, it is a ceremonial structure that is round and partly underground. A kiva is used by Puebloans for rites and political meetings, many of them associated with the kachina belief system. But in a deeper meaning, the kiva represents the point where the Hopi people first emerged from darkness to light.

Egahi and Shadow Dancer understood that creation of the constellation deep inside the cave was beyond chance or coincidence nor was the carving of the Hopi kiva a subtle clue.

Bidding farewell and with a nod of gratitude, Jesse and the wayas parted. Soaring into the heavens, Jesse's final message to Egahi and Shadow Dancer, "Follow the stars!"

Chapter Six

AS ABOVE, SO BELOW

There is a world under the earth made of magic and mystery. It holds the consciousness of nature's connection to all living things.

Pausing after an undetermined length of travel, Egahi and Shadow Dancer stretched out, belly flush against the cool earth. The usual sounds in the forest were dim and distant. In their repose, their attention shifted to an industry of enterprising elements producing signals far beyond the wayas comprehension. The vibrations emanating from the subterranean world were powerful enough to suck them into a vortex of curious obsession.

"My instincts tell me that we are amidst a complex conversation that I cannot decode," said the baffled Egahi.

"There is a story being told," declared the frustrated Shadow Dancer with a furrowed brow. "And I don't understand this language of vibrations."

Their keen sense of smell could neither detect the direction nor the origin of the unfamiliar energy below them. Circling the area in a frenzy, they realized that they were incapable of unraveling the mystery. In growing agitation, a howling Shadow Dancer transmitted an invocation, a vibrational S.O.S. out to the universe.

An immediate telepathic response emitted from a singular mushroom was for them was startling. Positioned at the trunk of an ancient tree rested a chanterelle mushroom, golden orange, with gills of forked ridges running down the firm and solid stem. With the plume of an incandescent tail of a graceful beta fish, the messenger began, "Eavesdropping, eh? Befuddled about the underground chatter, are we? I am Puhpowee[5], here to serve your needs. I am a mycorrhizal mushroom. I'm not an animal—I'm not a vegetable, something in between."

The wayas awkwardly introduced themselves, while still caught in a web of bewilderment. "I rightfully boast of symbiotic relationship with the trees that live in this habitat, especially Pine, Douglas Fir and Hemlock Spruce. We are the superheroes. Our species of organism is of the kingdom, Fungi.[6] Our powers can fight cancer, clean up pollution, and a few not so good effects on the human people types. In our habitat, we're all pretty good buddies, as above, so below. We have our own interdependent systems of nourishing, rescuing, healing and communicating, as you do above the earth."

Puhpowee continued, "The Earth is far more alive than humans know, although a few are becoming a wee bit smarter. The rich ecosystem beneath is almost twice the size of that found in all the world's oceans. Despite extreme heat, no light, minuscule nutrition and intense pressure, scientists estimate this subterranean biosphere is teeming with between fifteen billion and twenty-three billion tons of microorganisms, hundreds of times the combined weight of every human on the planet."

In the guise of a snooty professor, Puhpowee stated, "Many species, especially humans, remain perplexed of such mysteries. Our deep secrets may reveal how life and the planet Earth co-evolved. It is rumored that some of the findings enter the realm of philosophy and exobiology, you know, the study of extraterrestrial life." And, with a chuckle Puhpowee added, "Many earthlings are searching for some cosmetic filly-folly façade for answers. We are the majestic wizardry of earth alchemy. Our species holds the consciousness of nature's connection to all living things. We can heal the planet, build the future—our world is fantastic."

Without surrendering a moment for Egahi or Shadow Dancer to respond, there was a sigh, "Your mission is quite a distraction to the elements, indeed! Lots of jibber-jabber in subterranean regions—the networks are simply sizzling with the buzz. The message to you from the underground is, *keep an eye out for shards... stone and fire, stone and fire, stone and fire...*"

Puhpowee repeated the phrase over and over, as if in a daze. Then with an abrupt snicker said, "Remember me as a fun guy."

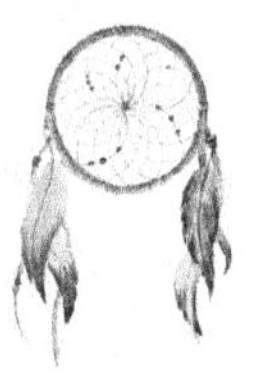

Chapter Seven

MIKO RETURNS

"Black hole" in popular culture is the ultimate metaphor for an invisible destroyer.[7]

Egahi and Shadow Dancer sensed that the trail was indeed warm as they continued their mystical quest to locate *sipapu*, the portal to *Heart Spirit*. This awareness motivated them onward, deeper and deeper into the undergrowth where lush mosses intertwined with the mesh of vines climbing on the barks of ancient trees. The waning crescent moon played peek-a-boo behind briskly moving clouds. The day had been long. It was, at last, time for them to signal to the creatures in the region that they were staking a claim. After releasing a few haunting howls to mark their territory, Shadow Dancer and Egahi settled in. Following a playful paw rub across a cheek and a couple of very wide mouth yawns, their eyes closed.

Egahi and Shadow Dancer slipped into a well deserved slumber. Nightfall perennially beckons the sounds of screeching owls, a hungry hedgehog, the raspy bark of a magpie and the cries of a bobcat. The courtship chatter of wooing birds, chirp of crickets, croaking frogs, as well as the intermittent flashes of fireflies were conspicuously off the radar. A hush spread across the woodland, as if the whole world had nodded off.

In the intense absence of sound, the wayas were visited by Miko, the Choctaw medicine woman from the Astral Convergence. In dreamtime, she stood amid an atmospheric fog akin to an aurora borealis. Dressed in archaic regalia of buckskin and a mantle of turkey feathers, she appeared in midair, forming subtle gestures with her hands.

She spoke, "Everything in the universe is energy." After a long pause she continued, "In the moment when a powerful star explodes, it collapses to the tiniest point. It forms a black hole with gravitational pull so great that nothing can escape, not even light. It is only detectable by examining the things around it. There are humans existing upon the earth whose stars have collapsed, holding in that space where the soul resided, a black hole. These humans sometimes look very average. They wreak chaos and suffering upon others, perpetuating upon the innocent such sadness as to rob them of the essence and properties of their spirit. The collapsed star souls do sorrowful damage to these innocents. Remember that upon the explosion of a star from the outer horizon to the center, the gravity increases, becoming denser. *Be aware of the dense energy homo sapiens. Beware of the black hole people.*"

Shadow Dancer and Egahi awoke refreshed to the chirping of morning birds. Flickering sun specks peeked between the leafy branches of the woodland jungle like freckles. A nearby ravine gifted them with plentiful fish and sparkling drinking water. Sagging limbs flush with blueberries provided dessert du jour. The cryptic message from Miko inspired them to forge ahead in a stealthy manner.

For many, boarding schools represented the first contact Native American children had with the outside white world. When they arrived at boarding school they were greeted by white teachers and missionaries who hoped to "civilize" them. Famous boarding schools like the Carlisle School and the Hampton Institute engaged in a brutal program of forced incorporation. The children who were many times dragged from their homes without the knowledge of their parents were denied the right to speak in their native tongue, call each other by native names, and were forced to leave the last vestiges of their traditional lifestyle, including their long black hair, at the gates of the school.

The wolves understood that the policy to "kill the Indian, save the child" could only be achieved if the *spirit* within was killed. Echoing cries of oppressed peoples, of helpless children darted before them in an elusive flash. Fervor was stoked like coals in a furnace, fanning embers for the soul of humanity.

Chapter Eight

LOST IN DARKNESS

Childhood should be carefree, playing in the sun;
not living a nightmare in the darkness of the soul.
~Dave Pelzer, Author of "A Child Called It"

Like helpless mariners at sea, swallowed by a mighty tempest, Richard and Michael were shuffled into an oddly different life. Signatures and official protocols were followed as an agreement for adoption was put into place by Gladys and Robert Davis and Diane and Robert Benson. A new world began of denigrating illusions of major proportions, as well as deceit and cruelty that would descend into depths of evil.

Ricky Davis was renamed Richard Benson and his brother Brian became Michael Brian Benson as their new parents finalized the adoption. This would prove to be more of an act of an *un-naming* ceremony than it was a legal process of *re-naming*. The family identity, Davis, was stripped away. The two young boys believed they would continue to see the Davis family and enjoy many more of Grandma's home cooked Sunday breakfasts. As the children headed down the road with their new parents, they fully expected that Grandma, Grandpa, B.J. and Elizabeth would always be part of their lives. But it was not to be. The sadness of leaving became a haunting ache that grew deeper and deeper in their hearts.

False promises that they would remain in touch with the Davis family was the first of many lies. When Grandma called to speak to her grandsons, the new parents made one excuse after another, blocking the connection. When the Bensons moved from Arkansas to a new state, Grandma Davis had no idea where they had gone. It was as if they had disappeared into the wind. She learned at some point in time, that while in Arkansas, the children were in and out of foster care due to reports of abuse. The Bensons now "owned" the children; their fate was set. Grandma Davis began to realize that the path she had sent Ricky and Michael on was a very bad one.

When the newly legalized parents were brought to the attention of the authorities in Arkansas for child abuse, the Benson family moved from Arkansas into Illinois. After breaking all contact with biological relatives, they successfully evaded authorities. Richard was home schooled which consisted of Bible studies and memorizing verses. He was shamed and scorned for his inability to quote from the Bible according to their demands and expectations. Eventually, he was not allowed food and locked in a room with no bathroom accessibility.

Michael, horrified at what was happening to his brother, experienced his own nightmare by being forced to taunt Richard. He was coerced into tormenting his brother by saying how good the food was, while Richard was being starved. The Benson's cruelty was not limited to attacks on his brother. Michael was psychologically abused, which would create deep emotional wounds.

One night Richard escaped out of his room and sneaked into the kitchen to "steal" some food. He was caught by Robert, who slammed his head against the floor, leaving an open gash. With no medical attention, Robert Benson took needle and thread, stitching the injury. Once again, they were able to stay under the radar to avoid authority figures.

"...After a while the Bensons' started to let us have it. They started getting meaner and meaner as the stay went by. Richard had to wash dishes and he didn't really clean them right and Diana found out and made me watch as she screamed at Richard and started breaking plates over his head. Richard started crying from the pain. Diana just laughed at him. I stood back in horror. I didn't want to say anything because I didn't want her to start doing the same to me."

From the Journal of Michael Brian Benson entitled *See My Blood:*

"Leaving grandmother's house wasn't very hard. She and our aunts said it would be great. That they would give us anything we wanted. And of course, a 7-year-old and a 9-year-old at the time said okay. We didn't know better. When we left with the Bensons, they seemed nice at first. They showed me and Ricky their house and friends. We loved it. We got to play all day. But whenever our grandmother tried to contact us, the Bensons said that we were out playing with friends. But me and Richard were there the whole time. The Bensons decided to change my and Ricky's name. We had no idea what was happening. So, we went along, and they even changed our birth certificate. We were now part of the Bensons. A couple weeks went by and of course we got in trouble. I was throwing rocks at cars. We didn't really get in deep trouble for that. They started us up in Cub scouts. They didn't keep Ricky in very long. They left me in it though. I got to cook dinner and stuff like that. But one time they decided not to feed Ricky anything. I thought it was a little strange and I asked about it and they just said that he was bad. I blew it off. Then they started eating and saying 'Mmmm! This is good! Too bad Richard can't have any!' My brother started crying and they yelled at him and made me tease him too. I had no choice. I had to. Life became even worse after that..."

Chapter Nine

LIGHTNING—ANAGALISV
(Ănă-gă-lēs-guh)

The Universe is a fractal. Whatever energy signature we carry will be repeated infinitely, again and again…until we change that vibration.
~ Paige Bartholomew

The entrusted delegates, Shadow Dancer and Egati, continued making haste on their daunting mission. Their hearts were bereaved from the ever-growing recognition of injustice of events: past, present and future. The atmosphere grew heavy, possibly reflecting the vibrations of misfortune befallen the many victims of ignorance, power, and cruelty throughout time. The feeling of sadness was pervasive. This leg of the journey led into an ominous passage, but to what purpose, they were yet uncertain. The cloud ceiling closed in, leaving only trunks of old trees and their vicarious roots systems discernible. Upper branches, as well as tips of tall pines, were of negligible visibility.

The soft falling rain was welcomed as it settled the dust. The offerings of negative ions from both sky and forest life pleasantly shifted the air pressure. It was then that the ashen clouds descended into leaden billows; the heavens morphed into scattered waterfalls. Although the coats of the wolves are tempered for a variety of seasonal needs, the sudden onslaught of water signaled them to seek immediate refuge. Retreating from the deluge, Egahi and Shadow Dancer burrowed into a formation that provided shelter, allowing a panoramic view of the heavenly stirrings. Well accustomed to the rolling thunder, the wayas frequently rendered melodious howls, as if sparring in a friendly joust with Mother Nature. Such sporting interplay was abruptly halted as they scented atmospheric conversion. Keenly observing the increased activity of darting filaments in the clouds they heeded the possibility of impending fires. The thunder rumbled, escalating into a mighty crescendo of timpani drums as in an orchestra gone wild. Primeval instincts pulsed through their veins inciting throbbing hearts and hyper vigilance. Peering into an eerie nightscape, streaks of lightning danced in frenzy. Before their eyes, the molecules and atoms of oxygen and nitrogen appeared. Ripping through the properties of air, like a cougar's claw protecting her cubs, lightning ruled the heavens. An exhibition of erratic flashes choreographed a visual that may have escaped their attention on their usual treks. What would have been visually indecipherable was now clearly in focus. Each of the bright strikes created a leader. The leader then sprouted off-shoots with identical patterns. The branches continued, splitting into more and more fractals. The piercing electrical charges held no sway for them in their elevated consciousness. As the way with nature, the course was finally run. Ever so gradually, the winds began to hush.

Egahi and Shadow Dancer appeared statuesque in the stillness, as their minds were churning the words of Miko, "Most of all, heed the great mystery of lightning. It mirrors the spirit of the universe."

Chapter Ten

MYSTICAL CRUMBS

*Symbols are powerful because they are visible
signs of invisible realities.*
             ~ St. Augustine

It was a dark, late evening. The roads held evidence of a heavy late autumn snow. The drive from Mokena, Illinois back to Kankakee was slow and cautious. A woman, named Palmer Tolly had invited a boy named Richard Benson to come with her, as arranged by the Department of Children Services. It was a visit designed to allow a close proximity to the legal proceedings scheduled at the Kankakee Court House regarding the case of child abuse. The radio was playing the song, "November Rain" by Guns and Roses, filling the air in an otherwise quiet ride.

Arriving at 13 River Lane, on December 18th, a twelve-year-old boy toting a black Glad garbage bag filled with meager belongings, entered the house announcing "I'm the new kid." After six months in St.

Mary's Hospital, and a brief foster home stay, Richard began his relocation with the Tolly family in Kankakee, Illinois. What was set up as a temporary weekend visit opened the door to a permanent home with the Tollys.

The new mom, Palmer Tolly, barely forty years of age, worked as a Licensed Clinical Professional Counselor. A psychotherapist in private practice,she had previously been a supervisor over counselors at Harbor House, a shelter for Abused Women and Children. Presenting Holistic Wellness concepts at colleges and university symposiums in Illinois, with her colleague, Renee Williams, gave her opportunities to research techniques in integrative models of wellness. As a pianist and composer, Palmer spent weekend nights playing in contemporary bands and combos for restaurants and festivals around Chicago. Approaching life with an unquenchable attraction to unconventional spiritual fundamentals, she was a driving force to teach and share the principles of wholeness of mind, body, and spirit.

The new "dad" in Richard's life was a man named Paul Robert Tolly, Administrator for the Kankakee County Forest Preserve. He had already raised three children to adulthood. Semi-retired, he was known and loved by family and friends as a congenial man of great integrity. The former pilot in the United States Air Force had earned an Engineering Degree and a Master's degree in Business. The fruits of his efforts allowed him to provide a modest and successful existence. Paul had arrived at a peaceful stage of his life. His approach to his endeavors was paying attention to details, yet he was consistently easygoing. His fair and firm fathering style was effective and respected by the new addition to the family. He often cooked dinner with a surprise in his pancakes, sometimes fruits or peanut butter that was always a fun treat for Richard. Paul delighted in his wife's musical adventures and demonstrated his avid support of her spiritual and professional aspirations.

Upon the arrival of Richard Benson into their world, the new parents were heading into unusual and unsuspected experiences. It was as if mystical breadcrumbs were scattered along a path, leading Palmer to something unknown, but destined to be revealed. Some of the crumbs inspired wonder and curiosity. However, other clues, more obscure, were entirely missed. It mattered not, for in some cryptic way, there would always be more breadcrumbs.

While on a spiritual retreat, Palmer dreamt of an indigenous male on a horse. The image was dark and shadowy. He identified himself as "Mystic Warrior." As this occurred before the computer age of research, she spent hours in the public library searching for some reference that could gleam understanding of the dream. However, there were no light bulb moments or sudden revelations. Years later, a summer garden hosted a Buddha statue sitting under a tree by the Kankakee River. This was an area where she loved to sit and read books. A face silhouette of an elder Native surprisingly appeared in her peripheral vision. Having no inkling of the event's meaning, she did know, however, that on some deeper level, it was very real.

Palmer grew more and more intrigued with an idea that perhaps the heart has its own unique and individual spirit. To discover if this concept was valid, both a relentless and passionate search would ensue. She was led down many mysterious paths, delved into ancient traditions, as well as theories of quantum physics. Pursuits to discover the notion of spirit within the heart led her to study books on esoteric phenomena from the Judaism *The Mystical Kabala* by Rabbi David Cooper and *Attendance of Meditations* presented by the Dalai Lama in Chicago, New York and Washington, D. C.

The proximity of her home to Chicago allowed her to attend classes with Sonia Choquette, a gifted psychic, author, teacher and friend. It was during a visit in the Windy City that she took the hand of Richard to lead him to a room with toys. Upon her return for the consult, she spoke these words to Palmer: "When he heals, he will have great medicine, Native American medicine that will help heal the earth." These words later came back to Palmer, as she remembered that at that time, there was no information identifying him as Native American. In fact, because he remembered his birth uncle, Mark having been in Italy and having a fondness for pasta, Richard had concluded he must be

Italian. He would later learn that his Uncle Mark was in Italy while serving in the navy. A few years would pass before the revelation of his native heritage.

Dr. Elizabeth Armstrong, a board-certified physician who practices acupuncture in Lexington, Kentucky, affirmed that in Chinese Traditional Medicine, Heart Spirit is known as *Shen*. She generously provided resources for Palmer to pursue the concept further and demonstrated a technique that activates *Shen* via an acupuncture procedure. All this new information was pointing to a truth that Heart Spirit was more than a curiosity, but rather part of a deeper spiritual discovery being revealed one crumb at a time.

Chapter Eleven

THE INVESTIGATION

A child does not question the wrongs of grown-ups.
He suffers from them.
~ Chief Dan George

Of all the erroneous beliefs that one can learn as a child the most damaging are those that attach a negative stigmatism to "self-concept." Whether the teaching comes from abandonment issues, abuse, or a perception of personal failure, the misfortune must be set apart from the core self. The deception, like an insidious web, obscures truth, giving genus to negative self-belief.

For Richard and Michael, the real world was extremely dangerous and even more difficult to trust. They existed in a vacuum of discontentment, in a reflection of the severely disordered minds of their keepers.

One night Grandpa Davis, Bob Davis, had a vivid dream. In the dream, his grandson, Ricky Jr. came to him. He told his grandpa, *"I can't stay here anymore. Help me."* Upon awaking, Bob Davis shared the ominous message with his wife, Gladys

Davis. They both knew there was a grave problem in Ricky's life. While the world was sleeping, his spirit transcended time and space, traveling in dreamtime.

March 19, 1992, the following was reported in the *Kankakee Daily Journal* newspaper:

> *Kankakee County Sheriff's Police and the Department of Children and Family Services investigate the possible abuse and neglect of a 12-year-old rural Reddick, Illinois boy. The sheriff's chief investigator, Barry Thomas, said the child was emaciated because of malnutrition, had multiple signs of trauma and there were signs of restraint. Thomas has requested that the child be examined by a psychiatrist at Mount Sinai Hospital in Chicago that has a child abuse treatment center.*

An investigation was initiated, and charges were filed. Michael Brian Benson and Richard Benson were removed from the home. Richard was hospitalized at St. Mary's Hospital, Kankakee, Illinois, for a duration of six months for treatment from starvation, broken bones, and torture. Charges were never filed for physical abuse and severe psychological abuse upon Michael.

The journal writings of Richard:

"Along with not feeding me, they started putting thumb cuffs on me. They started putting them on my two big toes. Let's not forget the board. Whenever they caught me sneaking food out of the refrigerator, they beat me with that damn thing until I was nothing but a bloody, whimpering, little boy. I remember one time I snuck out of my room to get something to eat. I opened the refrigerator door and I saw the shadow of Robert. He turned on the kitchen lights and knocked me to the floor. My head hit the corner of the kitchen counter and split it open. They sewed the cut up with thread and nothing to numb the pain that it caused. Then a couple of days later I was standing in the corner. I said something that made them hang me upside down on the door. The fuckers didn't realize that my cut hadn't healed and forgot that when you're upside down your blood rushes to your head. A couple of minutes of hanging upside down made the blood come oozing out. They shouldn't have done that because I was losing blood real fast. I probably lost a lot of blood at that time. Then came Christmas time. I didn't get no presents and barely any food. That was a time I could've used some love from someone that was caring and lovable. They even put me through home school. They were teaching me things that I already knew.

Stuff from the fourth grade when I was in the fifth grade. One day all of us went to a birthday party. They left me in the car tied to the seat so I couldn't get out. Some people walked by the car and saw that I was crying and tied. Fifteen minutes later a police car drove up and let me free. He took me to the station where they found out that I had been abused. They must have figured that out when they made me take my clothes off. They saw all of the cuts and bruises all over my entire body."

RESCUE AND RECOVERY

Richard Benson was admitted to the Children's Psychiatric Department of St. Mary's Hospital in Kankakee, Illinois, on the authority of the Department of Children and Family Services. Consequently, he was not present when the police searched the Benson house and arrested Diana and Robert Benson for the crimes against their sons, Richard and Michael Benson. The rescue was only the beginning. Treating broken toes, head trauma, multiple abrasions and emaciation dealt with the abuse on the outside but, the effects of such abuse on the inside—his heart, his feelings, his spirit—would take much longer to heal.

The original charge against the Bensons was cited as "attempted murder." Records of the case at the State's Attorney's office and the Department of

Children and Family Services reflected the severity of the abuse. The word "torture" was also language used in the documentation.

Initially upon hospitalization, Richard could not process food. He was given nourishment intravenously until he was able to eat again. His life consisted of relationships with the hospital staff doctors, psychiatrists, multiple social workers, the occasional visit from the State's Attorney's office and the transient relationships of other child patients. Surrounded by professionals around the clock, he was safe for the first time in a long, long time. The various workers, from shift to shift, got to know Richard and became his surrogate family. They grew fond of him and displayed kindness which felt so strange and unfamiliar. For the next six months, St. Mary's Hospital of Kankakee, Illinois, was his only home.

As the months passed, Richard became aware that he was homeless. His visitors were the service providers. Unlike many rooms of children in hospitals, there were no balloons, get well cards or loving family members. Though few, there were significant visits with his brother, Michael, arranged by the Department of Children and Family Services.

Richard's personal belongings were left behind. He couldn't retrieve his few Star Wars action figures and original Transformer videos. This proved to be a major emotional loss, as well. One of the nurses brought him some of her children's toys. Everybody was nice to him—a stark contrast from a short time earlier in his life.

Throughout the passing months, the staff "parented" Richard from day shift to night shift. One hospital worker, a counselor tech, reached out to him in a way that had a profound and lasting effect upon him. The frail, thin eleven-year-old boy slowly gained strength in the safe environment of St. Mary's Pediatric Psychiatric Department. Hyperactivity reappeared as he was nourished on hospital food. The counselor tech, a male staff member, spent extra time with Richard, introducing him to comic book heroes. This new introduction to superheroes was the fantasy of power and strength he craved. Filled with ardor, young Richard held the heroes close to his heart and mind. This began his desire to collect comic books. The hard reality of his world in contrast to the fantasy world proved for him both fulfilling and challenging.

Eventually, his brother, Michael, after several residential placements, became part of a loving family, in Momence, Illinois. Finally safe with Donna and Chuck, he was able to adjust to his new life while receiving counseling. Emotional challenges would surface along the way which required him to stand up to the haunting flashbacks that sometimes plague him. He now had a mom who nurtured him and a family who accepted him in ways he had never experienced.

The knowledge that their abusers had been caught by the law, gave the brothers some hint of fairness in the legal system. However, the expectations and hopes that justice was on their side would soon slip away. When the justice system addressed the case of child abuse committed by the Bensons, the criminal charges of attempted murder were pled down to Aggravated Battery of a Child. This resulted in the Bensons being sentenced to community service hours. The acts perpetrated upon Michael which forced him to psychologically abuse his brother out of intense fear and intimidation were brushed aside. The misdeed of assaulting the spirit of a child, was not listed in the legal books, and was rather casually overlooked in the judicial system.

The document of the case of People of the State of Illinois vs. Robert Benson, Defendant, No. 92CF states:

On the date of June 28th, 1994, the defendant, Robert Benson withdraws his plea of not guilty, waives his right to a trial and confrontation of witnesses. Entering a plea of guilty to Count III of the Bill of Indictment which charges the offense of AGGRAVATED BATTERY TO A CHILD, in violation of 38Oll. RE. Stat. 12-3 is admonished and persists. It further states, it is therefore, hereby ordered by the Court that:

Defendant be and is hereby placed on probation for a period of four (4) years from and after this date.

Defendant shall report to the Kankakee County Probation Office on June 27th, 1994 and thereafter as required by his Probation officer.

Defendant shall not violate any criminal statute of any jurisdiction.

Defendant shall refrain from possessing a firearm or other dangerous weapon.

Defendant shall not leave the State without the consent of the Court or in circumstances in which the reason for the absence is an emergency matter that prior consent to the Court is not possible.

Defendant shall permit the Probation office to visit him at his home or elsewhere to the extent necessary to discharge his duties.

Defendant shall pay all court costs accrued herein, including two hundred and 00/100 ($200.00) dollars as reimbursement for the services of the Public Defender.

Defendant shall perform 100 hours of public service work.

Defendant shall pay a Probation Service Fee of ten and 00/100 ($10.00) dollars per month.

The leniency sent shock waves through the hearts of all who understood the depth of the abuse. Somewhere along the process, justice was forsaken. To make matters worse, the brothers were informed of the verdict by a telephone call. Richard had not been notified or invited to the sentencing. The raw and dismissive treatment resulted in a considerable psychological setback for the young men; a clear message was sent to them from a failed legal system on many levels.

The aftermath would not be understood or even imagined for years to come. In the meantime,the caring families of the young men were appalled and confused at the leniency. This prompted Palmer Tolly to write a letter to the Judge who rendered the court decision. From his response it was learned that the case was resolved by a plea deal. Therefore, the court did not hear or see witnesses nor even see photographs of the abuse. The victims were not notified of the court date. What was called a "justice system," clearly was something else, and the children who suffered, were again victims crying out for judicial changes and reform.

Chapter Twelve

THE HEART KNOWS

If you have been brutally broken but still have the courage to be gentle to other living beings, then you're a bad ass with a heart of an angel. A sensitive soul sees the world through the lens of love.
~ Keanu Reeves

Richard's English assignment 11/14/1994:

Tom Turkey was a big turkey. Now, I don't mean an ordinary big turkey. No, sir! I mean an extraordinary, gigantic, big turkey. In fact, Tom Turkey was so big that he could feed 300 people. You couldn't even fit him through the front door of the house. I can't believe he's bigger than any other turkey on earth. People had to cut him into big pieces of meat. They even had to use two big ovens to cook all of the meat. After everyone was sick of the leftover turkey, they gave it to the poor. I could see that the poor really enjoyed the rest of the turkey. Now they're not so hungry anymore. Everyone had a great Thanksgiving dinner. And remember, only the lonely could enjoy such a dinner.

Richard's life settled into routines that helped him to grow roots. Some of the roots were new, like the peach fuzz on the face of a preadolescent boy, but other roots were surfacing that were deep and strong. In fact, they were so far-reaching that they grew from his heart and mind into the spirit of his past. On the surface, he was adapting to his new family and life remarkably well, but in the deeper recesses of his heart, stirrings of his early life still haunted him. Finally, gathering the strength of his true voice, he spoke of his longings for the family he knew back in Arkansas. He expressed a yearning to just be able to speak or write to his sister Elizabeth and little brother, BJ. This was an emerging sign of his growing stability.

Richard's brother, Michael, was living in a foster home in a nearby community, Momence, Illinois with Chuck and Donna. It was a good family, an older couple, with a foster mother who had a heart the size of Texas. A nurturing, kind person with an open heart and mind, Michael was encouraged, guided and sent to receive counseling for what he had been through. Oddly enough, he also lived on the Kankakee River. Weekend visits for the boys and spending time together at least once a month became a regular routine. There were notable differences in their personalities, but they played together and had fun. There was no question that the years they had spent with the Bensons cast a foreboding shadow over their psyche. There were moments while together that they managed to talk about the past, but mostly not.

As the winter approached, with holiday symbols everywhere, Richard ached to reconnect with his brother and sister left behind in Arkansas. Inquiries to locate the biological family by his new parents proved to be futile. Finding Gladys Davis was a greater challenge than originally thought. As a last resort, a call went out to every Davis in the Paragould, Arkansas phone directory. A simple message was left: "This is a call on behalf of a child who is searching for his relatives. Anyone with information, please call me back." But no one called. It was as if they ceased to exist—a dead end.

Richard's English assignment 11/30/1994:

I'm going to be buying presents for family and friends. I already know all of the people I'm buying presents for. The problem is what to get them. I don't know what they already have and what they don't have. The reason I'm giving them gifts is because that is what they like and I got them those presents. There should be no other reason except, that I love to give people things. What I want in my life is to have my little brother and sister back.

The response from his teacher made it clear that he had touched her heart:

This is one wish I would give anything to grant. I'm sure there are people in your life now that will do all they can to get you back together with your brother & sister. Keep the faith. My husband was 29 before he got to find his father and stepmom. We also got to get with his 7 stepbrothers and sisters.

When it came time for Christmas, Richard made a wreath at school and gave it to his new mom, Palmer.

"This wreath goes to the greatest mother in the whole wide universe. To the mother who treated me with loyalty and respect. Mom, I love you more than words can say."

Then, early one afternoon, the phone rang. A woman from Paragould named Davis said she was not a relative but knew Gladys. She promised to contact her and relay the message. One evening soon afterward, a call came from Gladys Davis. She explained that after the Bensons stopped taking her calls and moved away, she had lost all contact with her grandsons. Palmer told Gladys how important it was that Richard be allowed to speak to B.J. and Elizabeth and gave her a brief background on Richard's history since he had left Arkansas. That same night, Richard was on the phone speaking to his little sister, Elizabeth, and B.J., his brother. A reunion was planned for the summer.

And so it was, a car arrived from Paragould, Arkansas with Gladys Davis, her lady friend, Martha Short, with her fishing gear, B.J. and Elizabeth. Michael and his mom, Donna, joined the reunion the next day. The children were still young enough to display their innocence. Fleeting moments occurred when it seemed the separation had never happened. It was a time to just be together. Photos were taken at Olan Mills Studio. Palmer's friend named Helga organized swimming parties, and there were joyful pontoon rides, hosted by Chuck and Donna on the river in Momence. Private conversations between Gladys and Palmer disclosed some graphic details of the horror story of Gladys' grandsons. Such information rendered moments strained and awkward. Regarding the joyful siblings, there was no way to know what memories visited the children's thoughts. Notably, there was lots of laughter, but mostly amazement.

There was to be another reunion. Paul and Palmer Tolly took a trip with Richard and Michael back to their roots, Paragould, Arkansas. This was a return to where their lives began. Their arrival was met with uncomfortably hot and humid weather. The children were excited to be together again. Grandma Gladys was welcoming and warm to both family and visitors. By this time, their grandfather, Bob Davis, had passed on from this world. The Davis family would again have a reunion, which included uncles and their biological father, Rick Davis. Paul and Palmer Tolly graciously parted to Memphis, Tennessee. It was an opportunity to visit Beal Street and the restaurants of musical greats such as B.B. King.

Upon returning to Paragould to bring Richard and Michael back to Illinois, Gladys shared that her grandmother was full blooded Cherokee with braids down to her waist. She was frustrated that she could not find the photo she once had of her. Gladys spoke of a sister in Oklahoma who had papers proving their ancestry. Rick Davis, Sr. was an artist who drew animals and beautiful landscapes on the back of cast iron skillets. He was very gifted. Also, skilled at making jewelry, he made a stone necklace from a Native American burial mound for his son, Rick. Rick Sr. shared to Richard that he had the Native name, "Two Hares." Although the family did not appear to follow traditions of the Cherokee heritage, the necklace offering was a meaningful and significant gift to Rick.

Family reunion from left, Michael,
Rick, B.J. and Elizabeth

Chapter Thirteen

TWO BROTHERS–ONE VOICE

To harm or abuse an innocent child is an inexplicable crime and injustice on humanity. Here's to hoping we are wiser and better from this day forward.

~ Author unknown

As time passed and the brothers gained emotional strength, Richard and his brother, Michael, decided to prosecute the Bensons for their wrongs. Dissatisfied with the court's decision, Richard had an unrelenting need to sue the Bensons for the damage done to him. Michael, on the other hand, was filled with regret that he had not yet told the world what the Bensons had done to his brother. At the time Michael was questioned by the Department of Children and Family Services, the Bensons were earnestly working to have Michael returned to them. Fearful of the Bensons, but even more frightened that he would have no home, Michael was unable to tell the investigators what he had witnessed. As a result, he was not identified as a victim by the authorities governing the case. Having been forced to shame and humiliate his brother was an ordeal for which he searched without resolution to understand the guilt within. Living in terror, threats to his safety were always present. Sometimes they acted on such threats. Because of the horror inflicted upon his brother, Michael hid his feelings from the authorities. However, due to the progression of healing and the passing of a few years, Michael was ready to tell his story—a dogged urgency to finally speak out. The time for Richard and Michael to join forces, the time for each to give voice to their spirit, had arrived.

The process began when Michael wrote a letter to the Department of Children and Family Services (DCFS). In it he explained why he had previously denied knowing about the abuse to Richard and admitted that he was also abused.

Excerpt From Michael's letter.

"The truth is: I saw them do all of it to Richard. Another thing I remember is when Rob put the thumb cuffs on my brother's toes and locked him in the attic. They broke his toe with them. The constant abuse didn't stop until authorities stepped in. I am also writing because the Bensons didn't only abuse Richard but also me, but not so severely. That was never addressed in the case. I am wondering why it wasn't brought up. Is there any way to hold them accountable?"

The response to the letter from the Department of Children and Family Services was that since Richard and Michael were no longer in danger, there was nothing further that DCFS could do. So, Michael took his letter to the next DCFS status hearing and gave it to the presiding Judge, Kenneth Wenzelman. He did not casually dismiss Michael's effort even though it was not pertinent to the current status of the boys. The Judge directed them to bring the matter to the State's Attorney.

Their voices were ignited to speak out—together at last; two brothers, one voice. Richard hand delivered Michael's letter requesting that the states attorney further prosecute the Bensons for crimes perpetrated against him. It was an important move. It was heroic. Richard and Michael spoke out in their own defense. They were joined together as brothers. They had been children without voices but now their voices were found, as was their courage. The moment finally came for them to voice their need for justice. Once spoken out loud, their words took on a deeper level of reality. That is, until the State's Attorney' Office informed them that the three-year statute of limitations for such a case had expired. Richard and Michael deeply felt the pang of injustice. They had summoned their courage, their voice and their hope to speak truth. The District Attorney's response, in the form of a letter to Michael, rejected the petition. The charges had to be filed March of 1995, or within three years of the abuse. The brothers were never informed of these limitations.

The message was felt on the deepest level by Richard and Michael Benson, a crushing psychological blow. It was soon after these events that Richard declared that he wanted to be called "Rick." No more *Richard.* A significant symbol of his taking back his power, it was a beginning. However, the name he most deeply wanted to change was "Benson."

MICHAEL J. KICK
State's Attorney

STATE'S ATTORNEY
COUNTY OF KANKAKEE

450 EAST COURT STREET • KANKAKEE, ILLINOIS 60901-3992
(815) 937-2930 • FAX (815) 937-3932

March 6, 1997

Mr. Michael B. Benson
8598 E. River South Road
Momence, IL

Dear Michael:

A few days ago I met your brother Richard. He gave me a letter that you wrote detailing your knowledge of physical and mental abuse that you and he suffered at the hands of Robert and Diane Benson. After reading your letter I reviewed our records which were contained in our files against the two Bensons.

Unfortunately, the allegations of abuse upon you and Richard occurred between September 1991 and March 1992. I say unfortunately because under Illinois law all charges against the Bensons for this abuse had to be filed on or before March 1995, or within three years of such abuse.

If I can be of any further assistance to you, please do not hesitate to call.

Sincerely,

Frank A. Astrella
Assistant States Attorney

Chapter Fourteen
HOODOOS

What is the truth? This question propels the Heyoka into the sacred dimension.

Egahi and Shadow Dancer emerged from their temporary shelter to the aromas of a well soaked earth. They stepped upon soggy scraps of leaves blown loose in fierce winds, pounded by unforgiving rains. Negative ions had purified the atmosphere creating the sensation that they were simply walking on air.

The wayas were known to be most cunning in the nocturnal hours; their steady lope allowed them considerable ground distance. The lessons from the lightning patterns of *self-similar* gave them much to ponder and plenty of spirit energy to drive them onward throughout the night.

As each day passed, the solar energy intensified. The miles whisked away in what seemed to be timelessness. The moist, cool forest floor was gradually transforming into a surface of soft sedimentary rocks left from of the Paleozoic age. A diverse landscape exposing relentless erosion and significant climate change was upon them. Ahead in the distance were mountains, massive and monolithic, gently melding into an alpine forest resting in the lower flanks.

The sun was reaching full half day when the panoramic view of canyons appeared. Carved out of barren red sandstone, the landscape was tufted with sporadic clumps of wild sage. Egahi gathered some of the sage to arrange into wreaths to wear around their necks. She told Shadow Dancer that she suspected that their path would cross into some negative vibrations. He howled gently to the blazing orange sky, acknowledging her wisdom.

The heat of the mid-day sun, as well as the energy expended from the arid trek, mandated that Shadow Dancer and Egahi seek out a spot to rest. Surveying the barren vista that sprawled before them, they eyed red hills covered in burnt sienna and deep purple brittle shards. Nearby were coal deposits, glistening in the sun light, the remains of buried forest and creatures. A glimmer from the sun led the curious travelers to partially buried shards, made of stone with charred edges. The broken bits of flakes revealed an impression of curved grooves. The fragile pieces were definitely part of something larger, but of what, would remain a mystery for the present. The pair curiously mused about the message from Puhpowee. "Keep an eye out for shards, fire and stone..."

Miles ahead in the distance appeared storybook images of colossal stone mushrooms. Known as hoodoos, the columns appeared as giants, formed by eons of erosion, topped with a broad cap. Formed completely by nature, the spires made of rock and minerals ranged anywhere from five to one hundred and fifty feet tall. In the eighteenth and nineteenth centuries, black slaves of Hausa origin brought with their enslavement in the American South a distinct magic practice called hoodoo. The word comes directly from the Hausa language where the verb hu'du'bameans, to rouse resentment, produce retribution. Hoodoo can mean jinx, cast a spell on.

The wayas headed into the eerie colony of hoodoos. At the base of the chosen hoodoo they performed the common ritual of circling multiple times. The trampling down of wild growth gave them an advantage of shooing away snakes or other enemies camouflaged nearby. Wearing the protection of the sage wreaths, to cancel any bad *juju*, Egahi and Shadow Dancer hunkered down in tight formation, drifting into slumber.

The awakening wayas rubbed their eyes with furry paws while gaining better focus of the expansive lavender and magenta sky above them. Shaking off any remnant of sleep mode, they gave thanks to the majestic hoodoo that sheltered them. Leaving the sage laurels behind as a gesture, they continued onward. By nightfall, Shadow Dancer and Egahi witnessed a full moon. It appeared so large and so close to the earth that their howls seem to boomerang back to them from the luminous sphere. Species of cacti caste precise elongated shadows across the arid valley.

Wolves are quick to detect the slightest movement of anything in front of them. With a little less than 180-degree vision, unlike their prey species, they can see over 300 degrees of a circle. A scent signaled to them that they were being approached by a human. A lonely Kachina dancing in full mudhead regalia likely detected that the wayas were nearing, as well. Wolves have a special layer of reflective cells behind their retinas. It not only improves their night vision, but causes their eyes to appear to glow, often seen from far distances. The mudhead dancer had surely seen them.

Pausing from his dance, the mudhead introduced himself as a Kachina Heyoka. The Heyoka are sacred clowns, known for their movements and reaction in an opposite fashion to the people around them. He is a jester, a contrarian who can teach many lessons by such humor.

He addressed them, "In the days before the invaders came…we had clowns. Not clowns like you see now. And they didn't just come out once in a while to act silly and make people laugh. Our clowns were with us all the time, as important to the village as the chief, or the shaman, or the dancers, or the poets."

A subtle motion of his hand signaled for them to come closer. He spoke quietly, "I am Anihcak[8]." He seated himself on a blanket on the parched earth while drawing with his finger in the loose dirt. The image emerged as the same design of the symbol for Hopi kiva they had seen etched on the cave. Above them, the constellation Orion was vibrantly pulsating in the heavens.

As the wayas looked back to the earth a queer thing occurred. Shadow Dancer was now white as the arctic snow, and Egahi was barely perceptible in the black western night. Heyoka's trickery was at work.

Anihcak queries, "What is the truth? This question propels the clown into the sacred dimension. The truth the clown intuits is the interconnectedness of all life. We know that no one part is more important than any other part—no matter how big or how small—and that the tiniest change in one part produces a profound change in the Whole. The Heyoka knows that imbalance or blockage of the Life Force is the result of a person or group believing to be more important than another. So, we puncture that over-blown self-importance with sharp humor!" Next, he quickly gathered up sacred items scattered on a blanket and started muttering in a presumptuous tone. "We must get to Prophecy Rock. They are waiting for us."

Anihcak pointed to one direction while walking backward in the opposite direction. Catching onto Heyoka humor, the wayas followed in the opposite direction as well, post haste. As they strode across the land, the colors of the waya's fur reversed back to their natural coats.

Chapter Fifteen

ESCAPE

*Sometimes you have to completely fall apart and
learn to love yourself before you can figure out
who you really are.*

~ Author unknown

Puberty is an emotionally difficult stage for many
youths—but in particular for one emerging
from a complex past and thereafter being snatched
from the jaws of evil. At times, Rick had moments
of simple youthful emotions. He was always kind
and thoughtful, leaving notes about his whereabouts
for his parents. He enjoyed and excelled at guitar
lessons, received a certificate in scuba diving and
helped neighbor friends deliver newspapers. One
of Rick's teachers was impressed with his innate
ability to defeat the chess game over and over
without any prior instructions. His successes were
notable. However, with the desire and the demands

to be like other kids, unhealed trauma can be masked. The deeper the wound, the more difficult to hide the bleeding within. Gradually, it became difficult for Rick to feel safe in what the mainstream would call "normal." A dark undercurrent existed, undefined and only shared to those who could be in an unrealistic world with him. The only role models that spoke to him came from the pages of superhero comic books which were steeped in fantasy. The challenges typical of teenage years took on a far greater edge for him.

Acute suffering can leave inner scars that are sometimes slow to heal. Building an identity in a make-believe world might bring an illusion of power, strength and cunning to survive the evils of the world. Perhaps it seemed a solution for someone to erase "self" and become someone else.

It was a slow process, but Rick began teaching himself how to escape from the real world by living through his imagination. The deepening depression drove him to shut down from the family that loved him. This disconnection set him into a downward spiral, creating unrealistic and improbable mental beliefs and images, a desperate need to protect himself from enemies. He dwelled in two worlds, one of the regular school routine, and another imaginative world he hoped would give him power he never had as a little boy. Unknown to him was that his deception was in fact his greatest enemy.

With the assessment of Renee Williams, LCPC, a respected psychotherapist, Rick was immediately hospitalized. He had given up on himself. Wanting to be someone others could not harm, he in fact, was risking great harm to himself. With the right help, Rick could learn ways to unravel the web of deception into which he had fallen. Interventions Residential Treatment facility was to be his home until high school graduation. The staff was dedicated, fresh out of college, energetic, and zealously inspired. Rick adapted well to the routine and grew very fond of the Director, John Carr. He entered a new path to discover himself. With the professional support of helpers and healers at the residential facility this was also the beginning of a unique spiritual odyssey.

Chapter Sixteen

THE PROPHECY ROCK

Many are choosing a path with no heart, the spiritual path that was being abandoned must be rediscovered.

~ Hopi prophecy

Shadow Dancer and Egahi kept a lively trot to keep pace with their new guide, Anihcak. He had the ability to travel without his feet touching the ground. Yet, he moved his feet briskly, as if he was actually stepping on the solid earth. The remnants of a recent sunset left golden haze that fused with a starry sky, the interface of twilight. The wayas climbed down the canyons into the narrow valleys and cliffs forged by erosion with ease. Anihcak's signal cued them that they were approaching their destination. Demonstrating respectful obedience, Egahi and Shadow Dancer sat attentively at the feet of the Mudhead Heyoka who announced:

"From our Hopi Elder Vernon Masayesva, it is written upon a bolder in the Hopi territory. There is a diagram. It is called prophecy, so we call it Prophecy Rock. It depicts the emergence from the third world. See, we went through three worlds. This is the fourth one and it is standing at the edge of the fourth world—because by the fact that the predominant population of races have embraced a materialistic path. It has no heart…we are abandoning the spiritual path. And on that Prophecy Rock, the material path ends abruptly. The spiritual path just keeps going. I believe the path of science and technology can still be intertwined with the mystical path, a spiritual path, and a mythical path. I think it can be intertwined as they were in the beginning, when science and mythology was intertwined, then they separated. We have already gone through various stages of science and now we have reached—already going into another paradigm—called Quantum Mechanics, Quantum Physics. That is what Hopi always taught. We are part of the hydraulic cycle. We are intertwined with nature. We are not separated. We are connected to every living thing, and not just here on the earthly planet, but down bottom of the ocean, the cosmos, the universe."[9]

Shadow Dancer drifted closer to another wall of ancient carvings. Before him was a timeless story marking the passage into adulthood for Hopi young men. There were rows of animal symbols, cranes, corn stalks, spiders, wolves and bear paws, engravings created during ceremonial pilgrimages—Hopi Clan drawings.

One symbol roused his attention. Honing in on the image, he paused, thinking, *something familiar, yet not quite...*

Suddenly, as when a scent of a tasty morsel first awakens the brain, he knew.

Restless to share with Egahi, he signaled to her, "It is the image of the fire and stone shard we found. This is the whole picture." Revealed was a labyrinth unlike any other they had seen.

"Although we only found broken pieces, this must be it!" Egahi agreed with her companion. The etched image of deeply carved ruts formed chambers of eight sections. The path of the labyrinth artfully curved and twisted leading to a center chamber resembling the shape of a heart. Instinct, like the wind, was whispering to them that they had just found a sacred map of *Sipapu*.

Chapter Seventeen

UNDER THE BODHI TREE

Sometimes you have to kind of die inside in order
to rise from your own ashes and believe in yourself
and love yourself to become a new person.
~ Gerard Way (American singer/songwriter and
comic book writer)

When news of Rick's approaching seventeenth birthday reached the attention of the Tolly family friend, Jan, she volunteered to make a theme cake decorated with Star Wars characters. Rick was both surprised and wowed to celebrate number seventeen in such a spectacular way.

On a following visit, Rick shared that one of the other residents wasn't being visited by his family. Since his friend's birthday was coming up, Rick asked his mom to bring a cake for him. Although he was still searching for a way out of depression, his ability to care for others prevailed. It would not have been unusual for a teen to think about themselves, especially in a residential community. His basic nature was that of compassion.

Rick was making some headway with counseling, discussing feelings of depression and his pain of being stuck with his last name. The doctors advised against adoption by the Tolly family, as his experience with previous legal adoptions had proved to be a nightmare. Post-Traumatic Stress could be triggered by the mere thought of another adoption. However, bearing the name "Benson" was like a hideous stain on his soul, and linked him to the abusers. He was encouraged to find a name that would bring a good feeling to him, and legally change to one that gave a new and positive identity. With his fondness for mythology, he considered Thor and Zeus among other heroic figures, sometimes experimenting humorously with his mom asking, "How you doing today, Thor?" And they would both laugh. He was also interested in the name "Delious", after a singer in the pop group *All-4-One*. But this was also not the right fit. His pursuit for a new name would continue, sometimes randomly, but always in earnest.

One day, while working in her garden by the Kankakee River, Palmer, experienced a vision that she recorded in a journal.

PALMER'S JOURNAL ENTRY, 6/16/97:

"I am seeing the image of the face of a Native American elder. He seems very old, wise and

gentle. His hair is long—and details vague, as like one of those floaters you see after a flash of a camera. It was definitely a presence. It is a silhouette that appears in my peripheral vision, and I've been seeing it all weekend. It first appeared in the garden when I was planting flowers and weeding. When I turn to look at it directly, it vanishes. I believe that it is partly external and partly internal. Although if it is coming from my mind, it feels like it's outside of my mind—I wonder if it is perhaps some sort of spirit guide. I believe this is here to help me—but I don't know how or why."

The same weekend of the vision, Palmer visited her son at the residential home. Intervention Residential Center was perched in the center of a large lot with old trees. There was safe outdoor space for the youth housed there, for both fresh air strolls and outdoor activities with minimal traffic. A bright sunny day provided ample space for several boys running around playing paint ball tag. Rick was sitting alone under a tree. Rick and his mom remembered the tree, by naming it *The Bodhi Tree.* Sitting down on the ground beside him, following the usual greetings, his mom, Palmer, felt compelled to ask the question: "Do you believe in God?"

In a serious voice he answered, "I want to follow the Native American Religion." Surprised by his response, she expressed that she did not know a teacher for him in the Native American traditions. "What about Linda?" he asked. Linda was a Licensed Clinical Social Worker who maintained a private practice in New Lenox, Illinois. Her methods were both mainstream behavioral cognitive therapy and the occasional integration of Native American traditional healing. With her guidance, he was introduced into journeying through meditation and a form of art therapy to open his mind to the beauty of his spirit. He was very fond of her and reported feeling better after every session. Spontaneously and intuitively, Palmer agreed, "Yes, she has been helpful, but at this time in your life, I feel you need a male teacher." After pausing, she added sadly, "I truly wish I knew someone to help you."

So it was, that soon after her conversation with Rick, she stumbled upon an expired brochure announcing a convergence of Native American tribes to celebrate the summer solstice event on the lakefront in Chicago at Navy Pier. A telephone number was listed along with the mention of a Cherokee Spiritual Teacher. It was an eight hundred area code, which concealed any information of where the Cherokee teacher was located. She dialed the phone number, and then awkwardly made the inquiry, "Are you Native American?"

After a moment of silence, the voice replied, "I am Native Italian." The deep voice on the other end of the line was clearly no stranger to humor.

Palmer was stepping into unchartered waters. She explained to him that her son, Rick, was a

17-year-old who had been severely abused and was in a spiritual crisis with major depression. He was of Cherokee and European descent. He had requested to follow his heritage as Cherokee. The voice on the other end of the line spoke, "The man you want to talk to is Duke and he is Native American with some European ancestry, as well." He then added with kindness, "I cannot guarantee you that Duke will call you back, but I will deliver your message."

PALMER'S JOURNAL ENTRY, 6/30/97:

"On June 30th, the phone rang. It was a man with the name of Chief Duke Joseph Big Feather Schallmo. Through the phone, I heard a voice that reflected both concern and sincerity. He asked many questions, few of which I can remember. "My son Rick", I began, "has asked for help to follow the Native American path. In honoring his request, I am hoping you can answer my prayer for him to find whatever can assist in his healing." I struggled within myself to paint for him a picture of Rick in a way to inform him of the gravity of the situation— for I was yet to learn that Chief Shallmo was a man of great spiritual strength with the courage to help others beyond fear. I explained to him that Rick had been searching for something spiritual and his inner pain had led him into a darker side. He

firmly stated that it is bad to mess with the occult, declaring that Rick can get too close to things he shouldn't. I agreed. He asked me what does Rick look like—I was feeling that this person understood. I felt new hope.

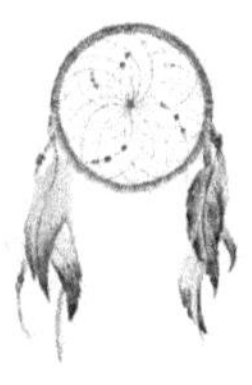

Chapter Eighteen

TWO FEATHERS MEDICINE CLAN

I will be dancing at the upcoming ceremonial Sundance for all the children who have suffered," he said. Then, looking at Rick, he told him, "I will dance for you."
~ Chief Joseph Big Feather Schallmo

The initial phone number to contact the Cherokee Spiritual Leader of the Two Feathers Medicine Clan was an eight hundred area code. Chief Joseph Big Feather Schallmo could have been located anywhere on the planet. The phone rang, Palmer answered, filled with trepidation. Nervously, she inquired of location. He replied that he resided in Crete, Illinois. Crete is a small township less than twenty minutes from the Interventions Treatment Residence and only a half hour northeast from Kankakee, Illinois.

The Two Feathers Medicine Clan has its roots in a movement of medicine men and women in 1876 who decided to form an underground Medicine Society that would recognize inter-tribal origins and share medicine and ceremonial knowledge with members of this society. Included in this Medicine Society were tribal members of the Navajo, Sioux, Cherokee, Aztec/Mayan, White Mountain Apache, Mescalero, Cheyenne, Ute and Hopi. Joseph Big Feather Schallmois the founder of the Two Feathers Medicine Clan after learning from a Navajo medicine man named No Name in the 1950's. In 1976, Duke began the Two Feathers Medicine Clan with the intention to continue the work of the Medicine Society and teach the hidden knowledge of the inter-tribal ceremonies through participation. This is not a mixing of medicine; instead, it is a recognition that there are originators of sacred medicine and ceremonies that are common to all tribes and peoples. Many in the Clan and the Society choose to follow certain ways that are common to Lakota, Navajo or others because that is where Spirit leads them, that is what is needed for them and those around them at this time, but this does not mean one way is better than another. Each must choose the path and way that is needed.[10]

It was explained to Duke Joseph Schallmo that in response to the question, "Do you believe in God?" Rick quietly answered that he wanted to follow his Native American Spiritual path. Chief Joseph Big Feather said he would prefer to meet Rick at his ranch. He further related that energy is very different in a residential home. Palmer scribbled down directions while wondering if the staff would allow Rick to leave the facility to visit Chief Joseph Big Feather Schallmo.

Receiving permission to take Rick for the visit was a slam dunk. The Director, John Carr, admitted his own curiosity about the customs of the Native Americans culture. He believed this might be a good direction for Rick to explore in his healing journey. The country back roads led to a large ranch beyond the town of Crete, Illinois. The entrance onto the property was marked by a wrought iron archway where it was written: *In the spirit of Crazy Horse.* They were entering sacred space. The atmosphere was indescribably different; it could have been on the other side of the world. In the words of Dorothy, "We're not in Kansas anymore."

They were greeted by a grey-haired man with a stocky build. He stood about six feet in height. The stout, gentle, yet compelling figure introduced himself, not as the Chief Big Feather of the Intertribal Two Feathers Medicine Clan, but rather by the name Uncle Duke. He appeared to them a bearded Native American Grizzly Adams, sporting a pot belly while smoking a cigar. His commanding presence brought out a slight hesitancy as they entered his home.

After a warm greeting, he shifted into teacher mode, telling his guests that, in the Native American community, everyone and everything was in relation to each other. We are all one family on Mother Earth. His tribe, The Two Feathers Clan, followed more closely the traditions of the Lakota People, but they respected and honored other tribal customs, as well. Mitakuye Oya-sin (mi-tauk-we-ah-say) translated from the Lakota as "All my Relations," a prayer proclaiming the sacred connection of all existence. The intention was to be aware of the holiness of life: human, animal, plant and mineral, planets, elements, forces of nature, etc.—and the Divine spirit that connected all. The birds, the trees, the stars and the spirits of loved ones gone before us were family. In the same sense, the mountains, the rainbows, the rivers and the dragonflies were relatives. Although it was a simple prayer, it was powerful, bringing together the wholeness of heart, mind and spirit with the universe. He gave lessons about the family of humanity being one family.

"I am your uncle, the stones are your grandfathers, the earth is our mother. Our elders are grandmothers and grandpas—that is why you call me by the name Uncle Duke."

Proceeding with a more solemn note, he directed his words to Rick. "I believe, Rick, that you are searching for something—desperately searching and could be turning toward a very dangerous wrong direction. Dump that dark side stuff!" In a serious tone, Uncle Duke told Rick that he believed in a positive and a negative side and the negative was not safe. He continued, "I am not your mother, I am not your social worker, I am just telling you that if you play with enough bad things—bad things can happen."

He stated he knew people who had done this, and something happened that made them regret it. "So, leave it alone. There is no room in the tribe for negativity. We are of peace, no killing anything, even bugs, unless in self-defense."

He instructed us to address him by his name in the Native American family, Uncle Duke. He suddenly shifted to his fun side and smiled with a twinkle of mischief in his eyes. In the oral tradition of storytelling, he mesmerized with stories unlike any that Rick and his mom had ever heard before. Many of the stories were captivating and laugh-out-loud funny. He talked of the Heyoka, who can ride a horse backwards or speak backwards to bring laughter in times of despair. Perhaps they were sitting in the company of a Heyoka that very day.

Uncle Duke then led them toward a curtained off area of his home. But, before they were allowed to enter, a cleansing ceremony called smudging was performed. Smudging is a tradition of wafting smoke of burned sage and cedar or other specific sacred plants to clear away any negative energy. Entering the main part of the home revealed a pristine artistic environment with many relics from ancient times. An astonishing mural was painted across the wall above a fireplace. The creator of the painting was a Native American artist, who had designed it in such a way that the light of the moon, in particular phases, would shine on specific focal points. The moonbeams highlighted meaningful images as the moon orbited across the heavens. The two guests were speechless, taking in the beauty and sacredness before them.

Uncle Duke shared a display of rare artifacts that held the history and energy of an ancient heritage. And, in concluding the visit, he affirmed that it was his delegated responsibility as leader of the Two Feathers Medicine Clan to pray, teach and assist in the healing of others in need. "I will be dancing at the upcoming ceremonial Sundance for all the children who have suffered," he said. Then looking at Rick, he told him, "I will dance for you."

Even without the full understanding of the powerful medicine of Uncle Dukes words, Rick's life would never be the same from that moment. The winds were changing in a good way. Rick continued in his treatment program at the residential facility, Interventions. Meanwhile, a new education had begun—learning the ways of his Cherokee heritage. Ceremonies bringing together Indigenous youths and adults for preserving cultural traditions became a natural part of Rick's experience. Endearing relationships were evolved as peers formed friendships.

The spiritual leader, Richard Pony Soldier Byrd, a humble man of spiritual wisdom, led a sacred pipe ceremony, canupa, once a month for the Two Feathers Medicine people. They gathered in Chicago, Indiana or in Kankakee, Illinois, at Rick's family home. Richard Pony Soldier held that although Pow Wows are wonderful social events for sharing Indigenous culture, his heart was in helping others as a ceremonial leader for spiritual gatherings. It was through his ceremonies that many lessons of the Two Feathers Medicine traditions were brought to the people. Richard Pony Soldier became a mentor, and a godfather figure to Rick, forever changing the course of his life.

Rick continued the academic studies in the school district system near his residential home. It was a special program provided by the local school. Updates of his emotional healing and school achievements were reported with consistency. The issues of his depression were sometimes expressed through art; there are some feelings for which there are no words. He especially liked the director, John Carr, who spent time with the youth by working out in the gym with them, discussing sports, informing about vitamins for good physical workouts, as well as other information. Rick spoke highly of him, with even a touch of admiration.

Cosmic support was reeling in the ethers. Earthly helpers, newly graduated counselors, reached out to young people struggling with identity, emotions, and psychological issues. Also on board were ancestors and ancient ones who had created a cosmic plan, well in motion, like a pulsar, rapidly spinning in the heavens.

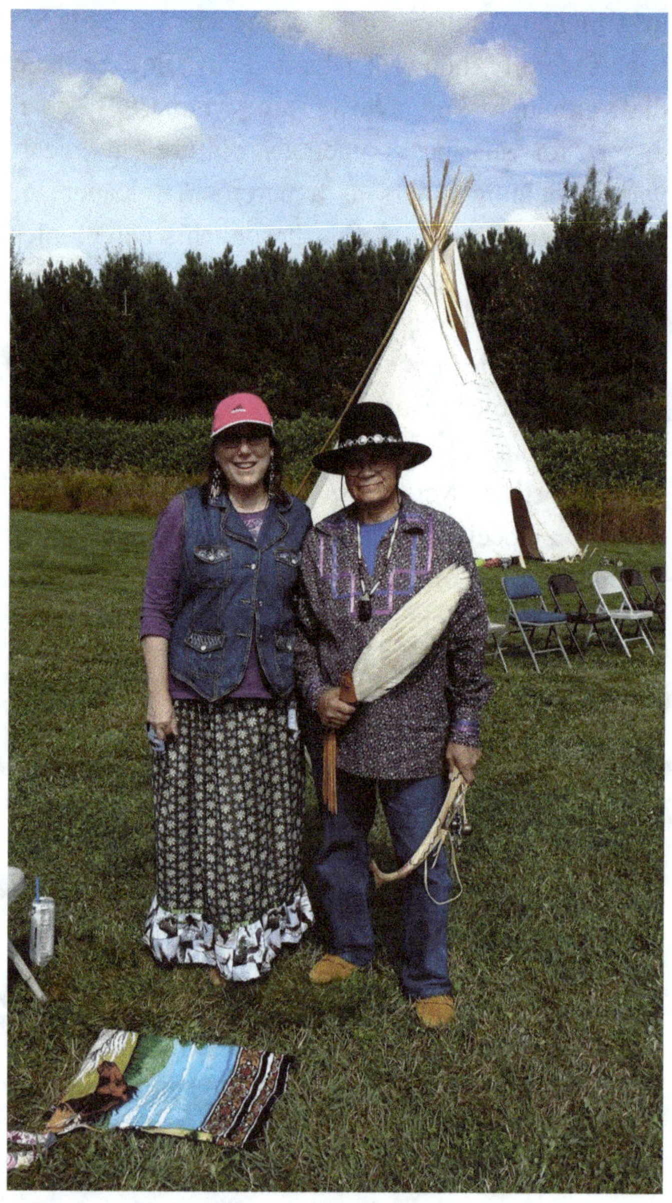

Joseph Many Horses and Danielle Lablanc

Chapter Nineteen

IN THE SPIRIT OF CRAZY HORSE

I salute the light within your eyes where the whole universe dwells. For when you are at that center within, you and I am that place within me–we shall be one.
~ Crazy horse, as he smoked the sacred pipe with Sitting Bull for the last time.

The scent of cedar burning fires filled the air. The hypnotic beat of hand drums carried over to the parking area from the ceremonial camp when Rick and his mom, Palmer, arrived. The two-hour trip from Kankakee to Spring Grove, Illinois was meager compared to the distance of those journeying from the Pine Ridge Reservation in South Dakota. The gathering was hosted by Joseph Many Horses Davis, (Cherokee) a spiritual teacher, advisor, ceremonial leader, Sundance Head Fireman and dear friend to Rick and his family.

His quiet and gentle demeanor often masked a keen sense of humor as well as a proficiency in Indigenous Medicine and ceremonial practices. Opportunities to learn from him occurred randomly; perhaps at a Pow Wow, a gathering at the ranch of Chief Joseph Big Feather Schallmo, Uncle Duke, a Sundance Ceremony or the monthly Canupa, Sacred Pipe Ceremony. Rare was the time when conversations with him failed to provide an important takeaway to reflect on at a later moment. Joseph had originally come from Baton Rouge, Louisiana. On the occasions when he came to share a meal with the Tolly family, they would sit by the Kankakee River to laugh and share stories. Attempts to impress him with culinary skills by cooking a pot of homemade Gumbo brought laughter and pleasant childhood memories to him. However, it could not quite match the Louisiana Gumbo of his mom and grandmothers, even with his sharing a secret family ingredient!

It was a warm evening, as twilight had passed. Joseph Many Horses had called tribal people together for a rare and sacred healing ceremony. Among those who traveled from South Dakota was Medicine Man, Benjamin Godfrey Chips,and his mother from the Pine Ridge Reservation, located near Wounded Knee. Lakota, from the Oglala Sioux Tribe, he was a fourth generation Yuwipi Spiritual Interpreter and great grandson of the famed Holy Man Woptura. It is documented that his grandfather, Encouraging Bear, also known as Horn Chips, was Medicine Man to Crazy Horse. Horn Chips had two sons, Ellis and Joe. Ellis became an intercessor and Spiritual Interpreter. It is said that he loved everyone with no conditions and had tremendous compassion, helping anyone who crossed his path, leaving a legacy of love. Ellis was father to Benjamin Godfrey Chips. The Lakota people believe his medicine is very strong.

By the time Rick and his mom, Palmer, had arrived, the ceremonies were well under way. The helpers were preparing to hold an Inipi, a sweat lodge designed to detox both physical and spiritual impurities. It was decided that Rick would be a fire keeper, assisting Joseph Many Horses in the heating and tending of the stones to be used in the pit to heat the lodge.

When nightfall came and it was between ceremonies, Godfrey Chips, Holy Man, walked over to Rick. By the glow of a wood fire with a summer moon lighting the night, the Medicine man took a six-foot staff that had been painted red, white, and black from the ceremonial altar and handed it to Rick, giving him these instructions: "When you feel troubled—hold this to the sky." He put both hands on it and raised it horizontally to the night sky. "Ask for help. You will get your answer." Rick's heart was profoundly touched. He would keep and protect the staff always, believing that, in some way, it would protect him too.

The final event of the day was a calling of ancestors by the Medicine Man. These helping spirits brought blessing and healing to the People. The Yuwipi ceremony comes from the Lakota Sioux. It is a powerful healing ceremony in which the spirits are manifested in physical form through the energy of the Yuwipi Man and are able to heal people.

It was customary to bring symbolic food items, new and fresh, such as an apple as a loving gesture to the spirits. Wanting very much to follow the protocol, Rick and his mom looked at each other blankly knowing they were not prepared for this custom. So, searching the car, they found the only food they had to give: Little Debbie oatmeal cookies, sealed in individual cellophane wrappers. The two visitors felt instantly that this was indeed a good find. Yes, the ancestors would certainly be delighted with these gifts! The lateness of the day and length of time needed for the return journey to Rick's residential home in Matteson, Illinois dictated that they head back. The Director of Interventions Residential Facility, John Carr, granted permission for Rick to attend the sacred ceremony. He was, however, a youth in the Illinois Department of Children and Family system, and therefore required to return that evening. The restriction did not allow time to stay for the closing ceremonies. Unable to stay for the Yuwipi ceremony, they felt a slight sadness. But they could not hide smiles as they imagined the happy response of the spirits to offerings of the Little Debbie

Oatmeal cookies. Off they headed into the night, Rick honored with a sacred gift, the staff from a holy man, whose lineage leads directly to Crazy Horse.

Joseph Many Horses in Ceremony

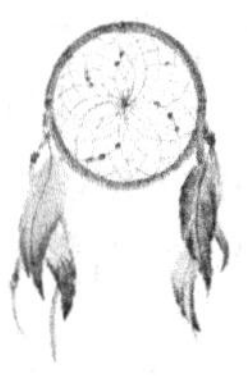

Chapter Twenty

MESSAGE FROM MAASAW

Egahi and Shadow Dancer ascended blunt cliffs into and out of hollows in their nocturnal journey. Lonely ravines filled with violent rushing waters contained by rugged walls offered no forgiveness. Crossing into the Mesa Verde domain, there were geological formations deposited between one hundred and seventy-five million years ago. The daunting mounds seemed to stare down the wayas, reminiscent of a noon time duel at the O.K. Corral. Pulses racing, they proceeded with relentless fervor.

It was approaching sunrise when the purity of sky presented a silhouetted image of weathered stone caverns. In concert, the duo paused knowingly. Words such as *rustic* and *ancient* barely described the aura that permeated the windless morning. With precise steps they advanced toward a figure of a person standing a few feet ahead.

A boy of maturity walked toward Egahi and Shadow Dancer. Dressed in cotton trousers and moccasins, he wore the hide of a goat over his right shoulder, leaving his left shoulder bare. A folded red cloth covered his brow. Bluntly cut black hair hung a few inches below his ears. He introduced himself as Ahote,[11] a local from the Mesa Verde. In a voice, not that of a child, nor the deepness of an adult man, he spoke these words, "Many of our First Nation People believe that we emerged from the earth. We lived beneath the earth. And it became time for us to emerge. Here we met the caretaker of the earth. His name is Maasaw. He told us this world is a gift to us. And we must care for this place. He said, to find your home, you must find the center place. So, we made a covenant to walk the world's farthest corners to learn the earth without feet and become one with this new world and to find our center place. After my people emerged from the earth, we were given a secret quest —to find the center place. So, some clans went clockwise, some clans went counterclockwise. Maasaw, the caretaker of the earth, told us to watch for a great sign in the sky. It would be a sign that we have reached the center place."[12]

Shifting his feet back and forth, Ahote anxiously motioned for them to follow him. He confessed he had been waiting impatiently for their arrival. His fondness for the wayas was no secret. "I am here to lead you to the Great Kiva."

Ahote imparted to Egahi and shadow Dancer that in Hopi villages, a Kiva is an underground room used by Puebloans, (also known as the Anasazi) for rites and political meetings. Among the modern Hopi and other Pueblo people, Kivas are a large circular underground used for spiritual ceremonies. His voice racing, he added, Sipapuis a Hopi word for a small hole in the floor of a *Kiva* and in many ways symbolized the most important part of many ceremonies. Kivas were used by the Ancestral Puebloans and continue to be used by modern-day Puebloans. Sipapu symbolizes the portal through which their ancient ancestors first emerged to enter the present world.

Ahote was assigned the honorable duty to lead them to one particular Sipapu. He held a youthful energy, endearing personality and in some cultures would be considered hyperactive. His countenance was radiant, his intelligence blatantly obvious. He harbored a love for all things in nature so passionately that such devotion could be described as supernatural. Since a toddler, he was gifted with a connection to all of the wildlife of the mesa. He felt a connection to the wayas, wanting to communicate with them, and communicate he did in rather swift discourse.

"Great Kivas," he spoke in rapid cadence, "differ from regular kivas in several ways; first and foremost, they are always much larger and deeper than kivas in the home. Great Kivas always extend above the surrounding landscape and are flushed with the abundance of earth's benevolent presents. Often, they include floor vaults which might serve as a foot drum. It is a large, circular, usually subterranean or semi-subterranean structure that was used by Pueblo Indians for important events such as ceremonies or political gatherings. Great kivas are one of the earliest examples of what archaeologists refer to as "public architecture."[10]

"Just follow me," Ahote said, with body language shouting hurry up, hey, come on.

The youthful exuberance of Ahote endeared Egahi and Shadow Dancer. They were not strangers to the playfulness and youthful impatience of their once young cubs. Upping the pace, the wayas and Ahote shouted in excitement, "to Sipapu!"

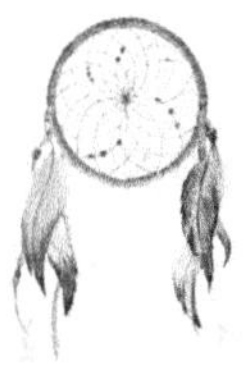

Chapter Twenty-One
MY NAME IS TWO WOLVES

"The beginning of wisdom is to call things by their proper name."

~ Confucius

There was a stigma for Rick in carrying the surname "Benson." It represented to him some lingering ownership that the adopted parents still had over him. The label brought intense psychological suffering to him, denying both his identity as a Davis family member and his humanity as a person. Attending a monthly pipe (Canupa) ceremony, Rick approached Richard Pony Soldier Byrd (Uncle Richard) after the ceremony and asked that he please give him a Native American name, petitioning that he did not want to continue to be Rick Benson. Uncle Richard knew his difficult history well. He took Rick aside and made arrangements for a visit to the Byrd home in Chicago for lessons in the traditions. Upon completing visits with his mentor, Uncle Richard informed Rick that a name would be given to him at the next Canupa gathering.

THE NAMING CEREMONY

On that auspicious day, the Two Feathers Medicine Clan members sat on the floor in a circle with the prayer pipes, as was customary. However, on this day, as they continued to hold the sacred energy of their circle, Rick was instructed to come forward. Richard Pony Soldier shared that the naming is a very important tradition among their people and he and other warriors had been in prayer asking for guidance for the spirit name to be given to Rick. Following prayers, according to the protocol, he proclaimed, "You have been given the name 'Two Wolves'." The assembled pipe carriers and the other members repeated the name four times together in unison. "You are Rick Two Wolves. You are Rick Two Wolves. You are Rick Two Wolves. You are Rick Two Wolves."

His spirit no longer carried the name Benson. In this space and place in the universe stood *Rick Two Wolves*, a young warrior of strong spirit, dignity, and healing. This was his family, and he was theirs. From this moment, he would always say, ***My name is Two Wolves.***"

Not long after this Rick decided that he wanted to legally change his name. The Department of Children and Family Services had assigned him a guardian ad litem named Sherri Carr, an attorney appointed by the court to represent the legal interests of the minor. She was a petite woman with a heart of gold who took her commitment to advocacy for the wards of the state to a level not seen often in court systems. She was known for being "a voice for the voiceless." The case was brought before Judge Wenzelman, who questioned Rick on the virtue of changing his name. Rick was strong in his stance. He wanted to keep Ricky Wayne, his first and middle name as given to him by his biological parents and take his spirit Native American name to be his surname. With pride and courage, he told the judge that he was a Native American and that the last name was given to him by his uncle, Richard Pony Soldier of the Two Feathers Medicine Clan. His mom, Palmer, stood by his side in the court and gave verbal support to his request. The name "Benson" was legally erased. His attorney then proceeded to complete the formal process: the judge signed the order declaring that on this day "Your name is now Ricky Wayne Two Wolves."

A phoenix from the ashes—the world would know him as Ricky Wayne Two Wolves. His heart had always harbored the kindness and wisdom of "Two Wolves." The "dark hole people" did not see, nor would they understand that the child they abused was always a beautiful spirit. More importantly, now Rick Two Wolves knew. He was adamant that only his birth family from Arkansas were allowed to call him "Ricky," preferring "Rick" by all others.

In the realms of higher consciousness, incredible, if not seemingly impossible events had been unfolding.

The two children, Rick and Michael, lost in darkness, had been transported onto a dangerous and perilous road. However improbable, blessed encounters with people of good heart and spirit also turned up on their path. This included: Joseph Big Feather Schallmo, Chief of the Two Feathers Medicine Clan; Richard Pony Soldier Byrd, Ceremonial Leader who gifted Rick with the name *Two Wolves* and Godfrey Chips, Medicine Man from the Pine Ridge Reservation. Joseph Many Horses Davis was a mentor to Rick. A circle of loving family, supportive friends and caring therapists stood by his side.

Michael, living a few miles from his brother, became part of the family who accepted him and helped him in his healing journey. Although his emotions would be repeatedly tested, Michael proved to follow an intensely honest search of his authentic self, discovering himself beyond the childhood nightmares. Becoming a seeker of wisdom, he was drawn to higher consciousness. The process would be difficult and at times, seemingly overwhelming. And, when the time was right for him, he would create his own re-naming ceremony reflecting the healing of his spirit. The choice of the name "Calvin" would be inspired from the comic strip *Calvin and Hobbes* by the American cartoonist, Bill Watterson. The choice of the surname was thoughtfully chosen, and to protect his privacy, in accordance to his wishes, will not be made public in this book.

CROSSING DIMENSIONS

The constructs of time and space create an illusion that the events and timeline in Rick Two Wolves life were distinctively separate from the events of the wayas. In the reality of a four-dimensional universe, such would be a truth: they indeed would exist separately. But there are other realities. The limitation of conventional thought, including cultural bias, may influence the acceptance or non-acceptance of the theory of multi-dimensional realities or parallel universes. The obvious exception, of course, being students of Quantum Physics, gifted visionaries and intuitives, science fiction writers and very imaginative children.

Since the advent of quantum mechanics, there is a growing acceptance of multi-dimensions theories. As the noted physicist, Neil de Grasse Tyson states, "So many questions we have about our lives make no sense in the higher co-ordinate system. Just as an ant cannot understand the plane of space "above," so are humans limited to multi-dimensional worlds beyond fourth level."

Wisdom keepers have roamed the earth since primordial times, protecting the sage truths. Teachers are proclaiming that it is now time to set forth the intention for healing humankind and the planet through the knowledge of Oneness. Such principles can now be seen as a fusion of quantum science with ancient knowledge.

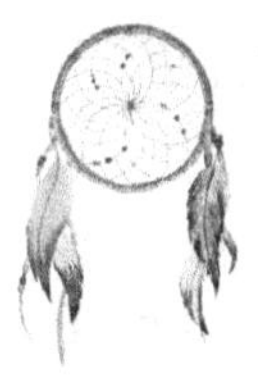

Chapter Twenty-Two

THE GREAT KIVA

At fast pace, Egahi, Shadow Dancer and their guide Ahote, crossed over rugged arid terrain. Arriving in a territory known as *Mesa Verde,* they stood amid massive blocks of geological faults. The twenty-five-million-year-old Colorado Plateau had been home to basket weavers, hunters and gatherers. The inhabitants lived nestled in alcoves along the canyon walls. Then, in the late A.D. 1200s, the people left their home and moved away. Perhaps it was because of a drought, perhaps because it was time to go. However, in present time, the area is known as hallowed ground, protected by United Nations Educational, Scientific and Cultural Organization transcending any National Boundaries as well as time. It is sacred land to Hopi, Pueblo of New Mexico, Navajo and Utes of the Southwest United States.[13]

"It is not much further," Ahote said, catching his breath. They came upon sandstone cliff dwellings, broken and worn with age. Wrinkled and pitted scars had defaced the outer surface, yet the structures stood majestically, with a vibe of spirits of ancient ancestors dwelling within the crumbling structures. A fissure in the earth's crust opened to a large crevice. Deeper and deeper into what seemed to be a bottomless cavity, they descended. The travelers suddenly grasped the awareness that this was Sipapu, a gateway to the Great Kiva. The steep drop into lower regions was precarious, but they managed to keep their stride and balance. The rapid plummet was somehow controlled, yet not in their control. Then, to their surprise, the trio realized that they were no longer in a free fall, but instead, were heading upward ascending to the earth's surface. This shift, for Ahote and his companions, was quite disorienting. The motion driving them was akin to a tornadic wind. A magnetic force propelled them upward and onward to the surface of the earth heralding a dimensional transformation. Stepping forward, they emerged from the cavity, a mirror or perhaps a re-enactment of the ancient ones emerging from inner earth as told in the Hopi story of creation. A bit dizzy, their eyes adjusted to the brightness of light and caught sight of an expansive arena of sorts.

Ahote, a bit flushed from the experience approached a Cherokee native standing alone. It was not certain if they had ever met, but it didn't matter. Ahote approached the man, extended his hand in a friendly gesture. The stranger stepped forward also extending his hand. He was of slender build, wearing jeans and a tee shirt. His boots gave him assuredness and confidence. A western hat shielded his eyes from solar glare. It was adorned by simple a turquoise hatband that held two feathers pointing downward. Egahi and Shadow Dancer nodded their heads respectfully to the man. He responded saying, "My name is Rick Two Wolves. Aho, Mitakuye Oyasin."

From this point, he would join the wayas. Ahote smiled grandly, addressing the man named Two Wolves. "It is your turn now. The lessons will provide for you what you will need." Then turning to face the wayas, he said, "I am a little bit sad to part with you, Egahi and Shadow Dancer." The eyes of the wayas rendered a sentiment of sadness as well. Ahote had completed his duty. A new adventure for Egahi, Shadow Dancer and Rick Two Wolves was now at hand. As he scurried away, he gestured pointing to another worldly vista.

As they looked ahead, grandiose architecture and natural radiance of gardens filled their vision. Orderly yet wildly free rows formed somewhat circular paths The wayas noticed resemblance to the archaic petroglyph, they had seen near Prophecy Rock. Egahi, Shadow Dancer, and Two Wolves discerned a sequence of chambers forming a labyrinth. The separation of aisles or chambers yielded seclusion of specific energies as well as distinctive colors.

Appearing before them in a murky cloud was Miko. She gestured, bidding them to sit while she spoke.

"We are in that space/time fabric of a dimension we call Unification. In this realm, there are no levels, there are no veils to separate or divide. Remember that ions, particles, neutrons, atoms of the universe are our relatives. Some are cousins; some are grandfathers, grandmothers, so on and so forth. Our unification exists of energy, a purity of harmonic motion. Planet Mother Earth has her own song. A particular pitch, tone, note, as do the oceans, trees and mountains and the heart, yes, it has its own song, its own spirit. This labyrinth represents the power to unlock and open the mystery of vibration to heal self, humankind and our relatives of the cosmos."Upon looking into the eyes of Two Wolves, she said, "You are the messenger, carry this forward to the rest of humanity, to the universe." Miko gave a subtle gesture toward the entrance to the labyrinth. Egahi, Shadow Dancer and Two Wolves, with both pride and humility, followed.

Chapter Twenty-Three
YELLOW CHAMBER
EMPOWERMENT

Tuning in to the Earth's Natural Rhythm[14]

A pristine atmosphere greeted the visitors as they entered the first chamber. A path dotted with raw stones of tiger eye and jagged yellow sapphire lay scattered before them. A resonance of 528 Hz, the natural frequency of the earth permeated the airwaves. It was not intrusive, but rather pleasantly audible. The resonating sound was not the product of any technology, it was emitted naturally from the elements within the chamber. "This tone," said Miko, "brings forth transformation and miracles; it is known to restore DNA." Egahi remembered that yellow sapphire helps in development and alignment of one's personal will with Divine Will. They strolled forward, inhaling the fragrance of Jasmine and Clover Bark hovering in the air.

Overactive apis, commonly known as bees, swarmed about showing no interest in the visitors. However, their presence was meaningful to Egahi and Miko. It was well known to them that many traditions believed the bee to symbolize community, brightness and personal power. To follow a bee was a way to discover a new destination. At this point, it was not certain if the bees were following the visitors or the other way around. Flowing onward along the corridor in a procession, it was as if their movements had been choreographed.

Miko spoke, "Empowerment is the consent to accept a reality of inner power through higher consciousness. The chamber of Empowerment is a realm for learning the inherent spiritual connection to higher co-ordinates. Many traditions identify the gifts of the Spirit as: wisdom, understanding, knowledge, courage, reverence and wonder. Embracing *empowerment* allows such gifts to reach full activation; visceral and real. Such energies are not just nice words; they are vibrant and alive."

"An awakening from within defines the very soul of the individual. It is a state of grace endowed by Great Spirit without judgment or preference," Egahi said.

Shadow Dancer rather sternly proclaimed, "The attribute Empowerment is not granted by earthly constructs, society, politics, family, fame, religious entitlement, or even holy people. It does not come from outside; it is from within." Shadow Dancer continued passionately, "The shadow side feeds on burying, deceiving, even banishing the truth. Often executed by manipulation and force, such acts do not reflect righteous authority, but rather reflect force over another. Even with trumped up morality, the end goal is to personally benefit in a selfish intent. The injustice of power over is rather force over. It is a sorry attempt to obliterate any notion of intrinsic empowerment by a controlling overlord."

Miko interjected, "Though masterfully hidden throughout history, unification with what is sacred, beautiful and all powerful does not rely on external constructs, but rather through the wisdom within the heart. The ability to claim one's spiritual power is revered in many cultures, both past and present. However, history leaves footprints of annihilation of many traditions not conforming to the powers that be. The dominance of Western civilization and society's conventional values gave sway to the banning sacred tribal traditions. Oral traditions were relegated to obscurity."

Miko, added, "In order to protect the essential principles of empowerment, it was necessary to go underground. Governmental policy was adopted that stripped First Nations Peoples of their power by taking away what nourished the spirit. Aggressively, the establishment of laws took Native children away from their ceremonies, traditions, and family ways. The actions resulted in both cultural and spiritual genocide. The assault on the Indigenous Peoples and Mother Earth created a chasm, disrupting oscillations throughout the universe."

Rick Two Wolves flashed back to the past when he was attending the Sun Dance Ceremony at the Shawnee National Park. He had chosen to sleep on the ground rather than use a cot, to honor his Cherokee ancestors who had left their footprints on the earth on which he slept. The stories told by Uncle Duke described the history of the campsite being a resting place for many Cherokee on the trail. The cries of children in the distant night could be heard a hundred years later.

Shadow Dancer stepped forward, "Remember to honor self. Shadow thinking can cast doubt on worthiness. The eclipse of empowerment includes non-acceptance, self-loathing and ridiculing one's self as a form of humor. Honor yourself in a good way. Strengthen your spirit, not your ego."

Shadow Dancer and Egahi paused to remember many noble warriors armed only with the power of spirit: Rosa Parks, His Holiness the Dalai Lama, Leonard Peltier, Nelson Mandela, Jesus the Christ, Desmond Tutu, Crazy Horse of the Oglala Lakota and so many more.

The scents of the Jasmine and Citron waned as they continued forward. The atmospheric shift was subtle. They headed onto the next chamber.

Chapter Twenty-Four

ORANGE CHAMBER
CREATIVITY

Egahi and Shadow Dancer walked in a comfortable pace with Two Wolves. Miko moved ethereally, with the ease of a whisper. Everything occurred in the present moment. The chamber itself seemed to be beckoning them beneath the glow of a tangerine sky. Their senses were flooded with the essence of vanilla, almond blossoms and oriental lily plants growing over the path. Jasper and sapphire stones materialized as they moved along. It was akin to walking in a pumpkin patch, only made of stones and vibrant orange flowers. Almond blossoms softened the earth beneath the wolf paws, bidding them "welcome."

A gentle hum wafted in the air, vibrating as 417 Hz, approximately pitch "D", on a universal musical scale. Miko related, "This tone produces energy to trigger changes, a frequency that cleans past traumatic experiences. Working on a cellular level, this inexhaustible source of energy allows transformation in your life."

"We are now in the presence of the energy of creativity," Shadow Dancer said, noticing that something was stirring within, activating his animus nature. "I want to run, to leap and to howl," he laughed.

In that moment Two Wolves revisited a past time when he studied with premier guitarist and instructor, Dave Stone. Rick's creative nature encompassed art, music, writing, certification in scuba lessons, collector of action figures, and kissing rainbows formed by a crystal prism.

"We are all artists of our destiny, our life, our choices and our thoughts," Egahi said. "The act of creation is both intentional and unintentional. Every idea, every thought is a process of creating. The 'thought' vibration is an astounding force. Therefore, it is essential to be mindful of our thoughts—to be deliberate with intentions. State your purpose and bring *that* thought into your awareness often—it is created!"

Egahi mused, "I fantasize about the joys of our pack playing in the snow and splashing in fresh streams. I overload my mind with ideas of beauty and fun. Whatever spills over is like litter glitter."

"My work is a bit more serious," Shadow Dancer confessed. "My purpose is to teach about the risks of creatively hiding the truth. Shadow hiding usually indicates the presence of fear. Fear is akin to dread and losing hope. Do not confuse fear with caution and alertness. Outsmarting a grizzly bear in the woods takes sharp awareness. We protect ourselves and family through focus and attention. Fortunately, our cunning prevents us from worry. Be cautious of interpreting the act of worry as beneficial. Do not obsess on possibilities that might occur. Focus instead on skills, aptitudes, and a cure to any problem. The "what if…" can undermine confidence and sabotage true power. It is said that we often create what it is we fear most, by obsessing on it. I teach the clan to identify their deepest fear, then to perform an "opposite" ceremony. It goes like this: First, a ritual is created in sending light to the mind for a "fixing" or "solution." Secondly, we un-create the wearisome thought by throwing it into a campfire to vaporize it. Remembering to be thankful for all blessings raises the consciousness. And finally, participate in a ceremony called the laughing dance. Frolicking, parading doing silly gestures while howling; this ceremony removes the shadow. That's pretty much it," adding, "I made it up."

"That is very creative!" replied Egahi. Her well-intended pun was met with a smile.

Two Wolves remembered a quote from the teacher, David R. Hawkins, "Recognized geniuses may be rare, but genius resides within all of us…. The process of creativity and genius are inherent in human consciousness…. A formula followed by all geniuses, prominent or not, is: Do whatever you like to do best and do it the very best of your ability."

Shadow Dancer admitted that encouraging others to take a risk is necessary, "Trusting undiscovered talents is a leap of faith worth taking. Some of our greatest gifts are lost in the Golden Shadow. It's like a waiting room for something great to happen, but alas, nothing does! It has to be freed, like the release of a thousand birds into the wild!"

As the aromas of the path waned, they arrived at a slight incline leading into the next chamber.

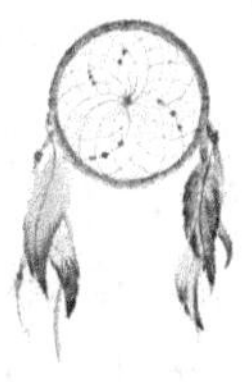

Chapter Twenty-Five

RED CHAMBER
BELIEFS

Egahi and Shadow Dancer moved onward on the curvy path noting subtle changes in energy. It was a gentle transition. The air of was aglow with red reflections from mounds of flaming bushes of aromatic foliage with clusters of scarlet flowers. The essence of patchouli leaves drifted about as they walked past pebbles of obsidian, tourmaline and bloodstones.

"Bloodstones are respected for grounding and protection as well as properties to heighten intuition and increase creativity," said Shadow Dancer. "They certainly are plentiful here."

The presence of sailing dragonflies was a clear indicator that many spirit eyes were around them. Miko spoke, "In the Hopi and Pueblo tribes, the dragonfly is considered to be a medicine animal, associated with healing and transformation.

Dragonflies themselves transform from aquatic nymphs to airborne adults, so they are often thought to represent change in our own self-realization, a change that's rooted in one's mental and emotional maturity. To our Navajo family, the dragonfly is a symbol of water, and the image frequently appears in sacred sand paintings to represent the element of water. In Plains Indian traditions, dragonflies are symbols of protection or even invincibility."

As the agile fliers passed by, a single dragonfly with iridescent wings lit on the hand of Two Wolves. He remained very still as he thought back to a Sundance ceremony, he attended around the year 2000. While the Sundancers were in the circle dancing, a mega-swarm of dragonflies entered the circle to join the dancers. At the end of that round, they flew away, returning several times to repeat the same phenomena. Two Wolves was speechless as he and the camp witnessed the dancers, and the dragonflies dance together in the sacred ceremony. It is a legendary story shared over and over by those who had attended.

Thoughtfully, Two Wolves shared some personal feelings, "Not all of my life has been easy, and I have made some mistakes along the way," he confessed. "I do not know what to believe about myself."

Miko touched the heart area of Two Wolves, saying, "You have been searching to be loved most of your life. Your proximity with the Dark Hole people brought you to the brink of an abyss.

Indeed, their star had collapsed—yours did not!" she said emphatically, "Throughout your life, your courage has been strong, your heart very kind."Helping him to remember, she continued, "Do you recall saving wolf spiders by taking them off to the woods, rescuing an infant rabbit lost from its mother, requesting birthday cakes for those with no family, even wishing that you could serve the biggest turkey ever to homeless for Thanksgiving? Rick Two Wolves, your spirit is pure." With that he stepped back holding his head a bit higher.

He remembered his visits with a healer named Jan Bell. She was a skilled energy worker, having studied advanced courses at the Barbara Brennen School of Energy. Two Wolves was delighted to schedule a visit with her for calibrations of his energy centers. His knowledge and appreciation of spiritual energy evolved through his sessions with her.

Two Wolves quickly felt the subtle changes in the air with the vibration of the note "C" permeating from the active bees feasting on nectar. "I suddenly feel free, free of negative beliefs that have shadowed me throughout my life," he said.

Miko explained, "This frequency releases energy and has beneficial effects on feelings of guilt, while enhancing one's ability to accept responsibility to always do better. The resonance 396HZ promotes the release of unconscious blockages, negative beliefs and ideas that have led to your current situations."

Our beliefs form the principal roots of our consciousness. Beliefs exist as tiny inclinations or as solid granite. Awareness of *thought* is helpful in moving upward in consciousness. The more benevolent the idea: joy, peace, grace, compassion, and love; the higher the frequency."

Shadow Dancer was known as a great teacher on dispelling the denser energetic frequencies, such as greed, shame, fear, guilt, jealousy, and selfish ego. "The density of energy can identify as a negative, or shadow belief," he said.

Miko continued, "The word 'believe' has a chaotic history. Beginning as 'manju' in Sanskrit which meant 'pleasing to the desires', the word was introduced into Southern Russia or in what is now Turkey. As land hungry farmers were seeking new territory, the language they brought spread into Europe. There the word evolved into 'leubh' which meant 'to care or approve of.' One of the derivations included 'lufu', which meant love. So, the word *believe* is the descendant of an ancient word for love which included such meanings as desire, approval, and permission."

Egahi pondered, "How different would our beliefs be if they were mental constructs of only love, approval, and the heart's desire? It as a pure and positive concept on which to build a new self-image. Using this approach can open the door to becoming who we are meant to be."

Shadow Dancer nodded, then spoke, "Our beliefs

must pass through the shadow self. This is a way to examine if they are valid. Thoughts of self-doubt, false humility and self-trickery are definite warning signs. Such self-deception often leads to self-destruction, including addiction, prejudice towards others, lack of empathy, and lack of compassion."

Egahi, "As we evolve, we ascend above denser energies. This allows discernment to recognize false beliefs from truth."

On a parchment was this message:

Maybe the journey isn't so much about
BECOMING anything.

Maybe it's about UN-BECOMING everything
that isn't really you...

So you can be who you were meant to be
in the first place.

Chapter Twenty-Six

GREEN CHAMBER
UNCONDITIONAL LOVE

A slight incline, serving as a foyer, introduced the next chamber. An obtuse curve led into another turn, heading them back parallel to the previous path, a U-turn of sorts, characteristic of labyrinths. The fragrance of musk was clinging to their auras. Ancient civilizations regarded musk as a sacred entity. Owning properties that bring relief from anxiety, stress, and nervous irritation, musk is known to promote clarity and calmness. The observance of a super abundance of ladybugs, along with an occasional dragonfly soaring past, hinted of an ambient ecosystem for a variety of life forms. Butterflies also swarmed around, wearing wings of every color of the rainbow.

Thick bushes, with crowded green leaves imposing upon slender stems were crowned with radiant roses emitting an intoxicating aroma. The guests were momentarily subdued and very close to giddy. The aromatic scents were not designed for the visitors, not primarily, but rather were purposed to attract bees and other insects for reproduction. The grand smorgasbord of flora provided well for lustful bugs and wee leggy creatures.

Floating atmospheric waves, akin to the aurora borealis, enveloped the new chamber. Egahi and Shadow Dancer had previously witnessed a similar phenomenon while in deep sleep during an early phase of the journey. Only this time, the wayas were not in dream time, they were wide awake.

Sounds floated about, as if somehow struggling to escape from the mist. The barely audible tonal resonance of 639 Hz gradually swelled into a modest crescendo. The guttural to lofty pitches formed a melodic sequence that brought tears to Egahi's eyes. Notes of a native flute hauntingly drifted through the air, rendering song of powerful properties: vibrations of self-love and compassion for others. In the oral tradition, passed from generation to generation, a flute is a sacred gift from the Great Spirit for ceremonial purposes and for healing. In this moment, in this chamber, the synergy of breath, wood and vibration realized its higher and greater purpose.

Egahi tried to speak, but the tears in her eyes said more than words. "These are tears of joy," she finally said. "My heart is so full." She knew that this feeling was not from her mind, but purely from the heart.

On the path before them was an ethereal figure, resembling the conventional image of an angel. There were no actual wings, but rather a light emitted that took the shape of wings. The curious travelers paused, waited for what was to happen next when a voice from the being spoke.

"Do not underestimate the power and privilege of being human. With one choice, our destiny as angels is decreed. Humans, on the other hand, have the responsibility of free will, over and over. It is a struggle for some, so often misunderstood and dismissed by others. Love is *goodness* generated and re-generated by the power of free will. Unconditional love can be described as loving beyond limitation, situation, or circumstance and without the expectation of return. Loving without reason, the opening of the heart is a foremost sacred honor bestowed upon humans. It gives them an immortality few can understand." Then the angel disappeared.

"In the consciousness of self-love, the vibrations are of the highest frequencies—no density whatsoever!" Egahi exclaimed. Miko reached over to Two Wolves, signaling him to come closer and to sit. As he did so, the wayas rested on their bellies, anticipating the words that would come forth.

Miko began to tell a story: "It was a cold bitter winter, just south of Chicago. A man, who traveled on foot from place to place, was a survivor of much suffering in his youth. His current housing was decent enough and the rent was affordable. The only serious issue was the plague of bedbugs that had invaded the building. He had complained to the housing manager, hoping things would improve, but they did not. Even with efforts of professional exterminators, the problem was beyond fixing. His objections were not welcomed, conditions worsened, and on a January first, he was evicted." Rick Two Wolves stared at Miko in disbelief, as he recognized himself as the man in the story.

Miko continued, "He wondered the streets by day and found shelter in a budget motel, until his funds were exhausted. It was bitter cold. He walked and walked. During the coldest wintery months, a local volunteer outreach group, *Fortitude,* provided churches for sleeping to the homeless and they welcomed him. Volunteers cooked up hearty and elaborate breakfasts for the guests giving them much respect and dignity. But then after the meal, the doors closed until the next evening. So was his day-to-day living. He made his friends promise not to contact his mom because he did not want her to be worried. However, one day his mom reached out to him to arrange mailing him a birthday present. It was then, and only then, that he informed her not to mail anything to his old address. He finally revealed to her that he was homeless."

Events of a different sort were simultaneously unfolding. Like the strands of an intricate and delicate web, certain matters were energetically spun—triangulating from Oklahoma, to Kentucky, to Illinois. It begins with the friendship between two elders. Chief David Thundering Eagle Fallis, of Frankfort Kentucky, had been ill with cancer for several years. He held the distinction of being leader of the Southern Cherokee Nation of Kentucky (SCCNK). Members of SCCNK are descendants from the Cherokee forcibly removed to Indian Territory in 1838. The second elder, Larry Eugene Sellers, (Osage\Cherokee, adopted Lakota) Buffalo Bull Clan, arranged to travel from Pawhuska, Oklahoma to Richmond, Kentucky bringing the "Lowanpi" ceremony for the healing of his dear friend, David.

Invited to this event was Palmer and her fiancé Paul Osborne. At the conclusion of the ritual, Palmer presented the ceremonial leader, Larry Sellers, with an early edition of *Chronicles of Two Wolves: A Path to Heart Spirit*. It was warmly received with the response, "your son will be okay. Prayers are answered." It soon followed that through the assistance of James Riordan, who worked with Youth at Risk, the outreach services of Fortitude and Thresholds and Rick's mom, Palmer, the situation reached a favorable solution.

Miko spoke, "You have demonstrated the highest frequency of love. Your misfortune presented you with an opportunity to step into a consciousness of selflessness. You have reached Agape, the highest form of love, the love of the Creator for humanity and humanity's love for our Creator. Remember to honor and respect yourself,

Two Wolves. Your personal medicine is powerful. You must protect it, as you protect yourself. It is okay to ask for help. Answer your own needs, physical as well as spiritual and in so doing you will bring many gifts to others. In this way, you will know the proper respect, honor and love of yourself to share out to the universe."

She instructed him to say the following words daily:

"May I be peaceful as the gentle winds,
May I be healthy and strong like the wings of soaring eagles,
May I have well-being—like the mountain stream flows,
May others be safe and protected by Great Spirit,
May all others know peace.
May others be strong like the wings of soaring eagles,
May all know well-being, like the mountain stream flows.
 (Adding the words of Chief Dan George)
May the stars carry your sadness away,
May the flowers fill your heart with beauty,
May hope forever wipe away your tears
And above all, may silence make you strong."

And it was in silence, that the wayas followed closely, with noses to the ground behind Two Wolves as Miko led them forward to the next chamber.

Chapter Twenty-Seven

BLUE CHAMBER
INTRA-COMMUNICATION

Everyone was greeted by a vestibule, a brief interval that ushered them into the next corridor. Following a path leading to left, they anticipated that it would bend still again to another left. It was obvious to them that they were walking in circles, yet never on the same exact path. They were moving toward a center of something.

The view ahead of them revealed a clear azure sky. Aquamarine stones paved the way. Lilac bushes and a plethora of lilies formed an endless stream of blossoms, erect, as if they were a receiving committee. On a distant hillside stood cathedral-like trees clad in green and white bark. Leaves quivered in a gentle breeze crowned the tall lanky trunks of the Quaking Aspen. The graceful trees earned its name from the fluttering leaves, which gave the appearance that the trees themselves were quaking. However, the vibratory nature of trees goes deeper than mere appearance or illusion.

Miko explained, "The Aspen's roots reach deep into the earth, possessing extraordinary grounding energy. Indigenous and protectors of nature, such as the Druids, hold that there is great wisdom in trees, sacred beyond measure. Tribal peoples believe that the Aspen symbolizes clarity of purpose, determination and overcoming fears and doubts. In many folk religions, trees are said to be homes of spirits." Pausing, she added, "But here is a surprising fact. The tree's roots sprouting results in many genetically identical trees. All the cloned trees have identical characteristics, sharing a root structure."Egahi and Shadow Dancer's eyes grew very large as they immediately recognized that trees are natural fractals, patterns that repeat more and more copies of themselves to create the biodiversity of a forest. Each tree branch, from the trunk to the tips, is a copy of the one that came before it.

Shadow Dancer slowed down his pace to help Two Wolves catch up on some of the important facts they had learned since setting off on their quest. "Earlier on our journey, we were alerted to keep a keen awareness of fractals, a law in nature of patterns repeating at different scales." A recurring theme, Egahi thought.

A hum emitted from the quaking aspens transcended all other sounds and resonated from an ultrasonic range that was inaudible to the human ear. Next to smell, the sense of hearing is the most acute of the wolf's senses. They hear as far as six miles away in the forest and ten miles in the open. Wayas can hear well up to a frequency of 25 kHz. Some researchers believe that the actual maximum frequency detected by wolves is much higher, perhaps up to 80 kHz. The upper auditory limit for humans is 20 kHz.

With gestures akin to a maestro in the orchestra pit, Miko, waving her arms in the air, conducted the pitch to drop several octaves reaching 741 Hz. The tone, commonly known on the scale as approximately "G," was now well in the hearing range of humans. According to the Solfeggio scale, the pitch guides one towards the right solution to a problem. At a cellular level, the frequency leads to a simpler life as it cleans away toxins.

Suddenly, a strange phenomenon occurred, and caught the wayas and Two Wolves off guard. An echo of the thoughts they created in their mind bounced back to them, an audible boomerang. Thought waves were transmuting into audible sound waves. Each word spoken had a life of its own, a vibratory signature creating waves into the expanse of the universe.

Miko, observed their bewilderment and signaled that this was another "teaching moment." She informed the travelers that many of their ancestors already knew of this wisdom, the transmutation of sound wave from thought waves. She encouraged her students to recognize that more and more science teachers today understand the alchemy of vibrations, of energy. She smiled and told them, "Let us celebrate that such principles can be validated today in modern science and will reach critical mass by the next generation."

"Hmm," Shadow Dancer queried, "I not only hear the echo of my thoughts, but I can feel the vibrations of each thought wave."

"What an interesting chamber," Egahi whispered. The message was repeated. *What an interesting chamber.* "I do not think I was prepared for this!" Once again, her words resounded back to her. *I do not think I was prepared for this.* She broke into laughter. Then, at that moment, the echo stopped as quickly as it had begun, no longer repeating their thoughts. "I have learned much by hearing my thoughts out loud!"

Two Wolves questioned, "Does every word I say in my mind reverberate beyond me and into the cosmos? If every thought creates me, and this creates my world, it's both awesome and pretty weird."

Shadow Dancer spoke, "Of course, there is a downside in shadow work. We are not born into the world thinking dark thoughts about ourselves. It is learned. It is modeled and reinforced by lower evolved individuals who function in a consciousness calibration of dense energies. Feelings of shame, guilt, prejudice and fear feed the mind negative thoughts. Negative thoughts feed errors in self-beliefs. My greatest hope is that this mission will help humans to learn the power of communicating only those thought forms that heighten awareness and insight."

Miko took the floor again, saying, "Constructive and destructive communications to world citizens can come from many sources: parents, relatives, siblings, schoolteachers, coaches, ministers, religious leaders, supervisors, mentors or any authority figure. When the messages are consistently negative, and when the person is most vulnerable, a veil grows thicker, the shadows darker." She continued, "Many Iroquois Chiefs and other tribal principles hold that their decision making is guided by consideration of the well-being of others into the next seven generations. Imagine how different our society would be if we took responsibility for the energetic effect of our words, thoughts, and actions into the next seven generations! Children are among the most sensitive and vulnerable to impressions and often those impressions last a lifetime. Even as adults we hold within the essence and energy of our inner child."

The turn into the next corridor was a much shorter distance, actually only a few paces. To the left, then swerving in a snake-like move, they headed to the right.

Chapter Twenty-Eight
INDIGO CHAMBER
VISION

An expansive golden moon dominated the sky like a celestial dome. A twilight skyscape wore an intense purple shade melding into the closure of a blue-sky day. A variety of stones appeared scattered along the chamber, including Lapis Lazuli, historically associated with wisdom, intellect and truth. The distinct fragrance of lavender ruled the air, while a hint of balsam attempted to compete.

A steady pulse, as if coming from an orchestral section of celestial percussion, resonated963Hz. This was more than a frequency; it was also a rhythm. The tempo was infectious, bringing a slight sway to the step of the travelers. The frequency associated with the third eye, has also been identified as Pure Miracle Tones assisting in the attainment of sharper intuition and the gift of clairvoyance.

Two Wolves was both intrigued and amused with the sounds radiated in the ethers. His head and shoulders were bobbing to the groove of the rhythmic pattern when Miko gestured for him to remove his hat. She presented to him a cotton cloth of the color indigo. He wrapped it around his eyes, bandana style, per the instructions given by the Choctaw elder. She told him, "It is not outer sight, but inner sight that you seek."

Reminded of lessons from Yoda to Luke Skywalker, he enthusiastically followed directions. "Overflow your mind with what is beautiful and good. And what you visualize over and over will manifest as your reality. What you see hence forth, will come from the higher realms. What do you know, Two Wolves?" she asked the blindfolded traveler. A few moments of silence ensued. Then he gave a deliberate response, "I think that visions are like having a dream while you are awake but can come during sleeping. Higher levels of thoughts open the mind to best interpret the vision. There is no order of deserving a vision. It is not earned by rank, position or status. A vision is the occurrence of a formula, like a perfect energetic storm, but in a good way." Miko nodded approvingly adding, "A vision is unique to the one experiencing it. Most people would not admit to the experience of having a vision. Share only if it can benefit others." He then removed the blindfold as his companions smiled.

Shadow Dancer, in a casual manner, said, "By the way, in those moments that your aura is assaulted by lower and denser vibrations, visualize a protective barrier around you. In the light you imagine, no harm will come to you."

"Hey, thanks," was returned to the waya from Two Wolves.

In a déjà vu moment, he remembered another twilight sky at the ceremonial camp of Joseph Many Horses, when Holy Man, Godfrey Chipps, presented him with the sacred staff that would give him insight and protection.

The path curved to the left and then curled to the right as if closing in, shorter and smaller arcs, more or less, making a U-turn. Suddenly, they were somewhere beyond the earth plane.

Chapter Twenty-Nine
LAVENDER CHAMBER
ONENESS

A deep and guttural drone of breathy harmonies and dissonance floated in the distant ethers. The frequency of 963 Hz greeted the visitors.

Through teleportation, Egahi, Shadow Dancer, Two Wolves and Miko, arrived somewhere in the outer perimeters of space. Although the laws of gravity no longer applied, the terrestrials found themselves to be both surefooted and well grounded. Their energy fields revealed an aura of pastel crystal lavender. The sky was carbon black, punctuated by a meteor darting from point "A" on its travels to infinity.

Two Wolves, in wonderment, pondered a heaven brimming with constellations: the twinkling span of the Milky Way. Miko broke the silence: "Being vast and grand, the universe does not intimidate us mortal beings. Instead, it empowers us. Starting from the gaze, we make connections with the universe. We become part of it and we get to know it. Saved by a gaze, we are not at all small, not at all mortal, and not at all worthless."

"Is it true? Are we really made of stardust?" Shadow Dancer asked.

Two Wolves, who loved the study of stars, answered, "Well, in my readings, I learned that many of the elements of the periodic table come from a supernova," then he added, "even those that make up the human body. Carl Sagan, one of my favorite astronomers, said that we're made of star stuff. The carbon, nitrogen and oxygen atoms in our bodies, as well as atoms of all other heavy elements, were created in previous generational stars over 4.5 billion years ago."

Egahi spoke, "It is totally one hundred percent true. Nearly all the elements in the human body were made in a star and many have come through several supernovas. Basically, we are all energy bundles," she laughed.

Miko added, "That you exist as a body of energy is a simple basic fact. You are made up of seven billion, billion, billion vibrating atoms. That's a lot of energy. If a frequency is vibrating fast enough, it's emitted as a sound and if it is vibrating much faster, it is emitted as a color of light."

Egahi smiled, "We are slowed down sound and light waves, a walking bundle of frequencies tuned in to the cosmos. We are souls dressed up in biochemical garments and our bodies are the instruments through which our souls play their music."

"The traditional ways of ancestors have always honored our *connection* to the cosmos," Miko added.

Shadow Dancer interjected, "Sadly, any disruption of the spirit energy grid creates a chasm. When this occurs, the spirit, the soul within, grows dim, weaker. All living forms are hurting. The hearts of children are searching in dark. Hills and valleys that were sacred to ancestors are being destroyed, the water is polluted, and chemicals are poisoning the seas."

Miko added, "Everything is connected, a sacred web of life. Each event of a compassionate thought is fortifying strands of the sacred web. Most people have only a veiled understanding of consciousness. When plants turn its leaves to the sun, that is a form of consciousness. There is an animal consciousness. In the woods, you can observe their different levels of consciousness relating to each other. Scientists are starting to talk about the Gaia Principle, the whole planet as an organism, Mother Earth. Think of ourselves as coming out of the earth rather than being from somewhere else".

Egahi paused, then spoke words of Black Elk, Holy Man of the Oglala Sioux: "At the center of the universe dwells the Great Spirit. And that center is really everywhere. It is within each of us."

Chapter Thirty
HEART SPIRIT

Though the twists and turns were gentle and gradual, the path continually moved them onward. The summation of profound cosmic vibrations, a synergy, brought them to feelings of humility and empowerment as they entered the eighth chamber. A vista before them appeared of the Milky Way galaxy. Expansive and infinite, it was but the backdrop for the staging of an unfolding vision. Whether or not this was an illusion or was actual time travel back to another time and space was only known by Miko.

Miko, speaking in a commanding tone, "You are in the dimension of past/present. It is October 2nd, 2010. Rick Two Wolves and his mom, Palmer leave in plenty of time to arrive early at the funeral service at 11:00 a.m. for Richard M. Byrd, known and loved as Richard Pony Soldier. The Ceremonial Pipe Leader for the Two Feathers

Medicine Clan is now free of earthly boundaries, beyond physical suffering. News of his death stirs deep emotions in the hearts of all who knew him."

Before them, the scene appeared:

Rick and his mom, Palmer, are slowly eyeing every side street they cross. The destination to 5725 S. Pulaski Rd. in Chicago was achieved. Approaching the entrance of the funeral home, familiar faces give casual nods, a subtle but sincere welcome. The Modell Funeral Home is crowded, filled with family and friends. Palmer sees Richard's daughter, Jessica She Dog Byrd. In bereavement, she wipes a steady flow of tears as she stands with family near the body of her beloved father.

Miko narrates, "Jessica was twelve when Rick met her. She is now a grown woman with a daughter. Richard Pony Soldier adored them both. When Jessica was much younger Palmer watched her dance in beautiful regalia. That, in turn, inspired the idea to fashion a Native American doll dressed in the identical regalia. She contacted a family friend of the Byrd family in southern Illinois, who had sewn the original regalia Jessica wore as a Rainbow Dancer at PowWows. With left over fabric and the original pattern and the sewing prowess of Terry Althouse, a doll named She Dog, was gifted to her."

Two Wolves, Egahi & Shadow Dancer continued to observe. *Homage to Richard Pony Soldier Bryd brings friends and relatives from great distances.*

Old relationships are being renewed with exchanges of phone numbers and email addresses. The rooms are filling up quickly, leaving standing room only.

Miko, "The vibrations are accelerating exponentially by thought energies, higher frequencies swarm about as friends emanate gratitude for being on the earth walk with the humble and kind man, Richard."

Back to the vision:

Tobacco, sage and cedar is passed around. Rick Two Wolves is looking around the room, seeking his own space, reaching out to his closest friends in the room. Acquaintances he recognizes from the days at Uncle Dukes' ranch are sharing kindred emotions. Palmer is approaches the reception line, viewing what had once been the earthly vessel for Uncle Richard. Members of the Two Feathers Medicine Clan reach out to her with melancholy embrace, Candy Byrd, Richard's wife, Strength of Two Hawks, Chris and Nadine Culver and Cindy Crow Woman.

The service begins with prayers by Jerry Dodd, Candy Byrd's uncle from Tennessee, followed by native drummers creating an intense synergy of jubilation of Richard Pony Soldier's life on earth. A recording of "Amazing Grace" is playing on a boom box; many are singing the words in Cherokee. (This song was adopted by the Cherokee who sang it on their journey of the Trail of Tears.) "I'll Fly Away" follows as drumming and chants fill the air. Eulogies are offered. Richard is honored with the title "Chief."

Tributes and endearing stories alternate with the vibrations of the ceremonial drums, each round more forceful, more powerful than the previous one. A collective consciousness, the merging of elements created by the energies of deep affection for Richard Pony Soldier is coalescing.

Palmer, looking up to the left, towards the ceiling, above Richard's body, sees his spirit dancing. He is dressed in vivid and colorful regalia. He is agile, slightly bent forward, not because of age, but rather because it is the proper form of the dance. He steps vigorously. He steps youthfully high. It seems that no one else is witnessing the same apparition. The service is winding down. Hugs and friendship gestures suggest the tribute is completed.

Rick and his mom are heading to their car for the return trip back to Kankakee, IL. A gray cold October day, old streets and old buildings are obscured by the downpour of rain. Rick is a willing co-pilot, searching for the street sign to lead back to Hwy 294, going south. With no GPS, she tells him to look on the right side for the street sign they need to find, she will look on the left.

Watching with careful scrutiny, the wiper blades laboriously swish away the pouring rain. Amid this high traffic moment, a radiant light is emitted from Palmer's chest as a kind of starburst. A myriad of pastel colors, prisms, shoot forth from her heart area, spraying outward—lasting a microsecond." She says nothing, wondering, "Is this Heart Spirit?

The ride home is peaceful and mostly without words.
Miko directs the visitors to now gather closely to
review important lessons:

Empowerment

Permission to experience our true spirit power.

Creativity

Quenching the soul's thirst to communicate
through the arts and expressions of the soul,
curiosity and adventure.

Belief

Accepting individual responsibility of creating
a personal blueprint.

Unconditional Love

Nurturing love within to give to others.

Intra-Communication

Speak to yourself in a mindful way. Honoring self
through respect and responsibility.

Vision

The energies to see beyond the obvious
through higher consciousness.

Unity, Connection

Aligning frequencies of loving oneness.

Beneath the feet of Egahi, Shadow Dancer, Two Wolves and Miko, sprouted a variety of flora, rocketing from the ground in such rapidity, soil became virtually invisible. A floral carpet of blossoms spread out like a sea of effervescence. The surface of each flower manifested the structure of an electric field. Some details of floral anatomy appeared revealing the parts with higher charge density (and therefore greater electric force) along contours and sharp features, such as the edges of petal, stigma, and anthers. The geometry of petal edges, where charge density is high, provided spatial structure to the floral field, giving it an outline. The splendor evoked surprise in the spectators. Everything was more than alive. Images of oscillating atoms danced before their eyes wildly, yet with purpose.

All sensory experience seemed surreal: pulsating, invigorating.

Their eyes followed Miko pointing towards the sky and speaks, "The element of Ether, or Aether, is the celestial energy that fills all places. The Greeks believed it to be higher than the earth plane, a well known phenomenon like gravity. In the sage tradition of many ancient teachers, the concept of spirit goes much further than what is commonly accepted. It is the center of sacred space, the mandala of the universe and beyond. It is the pattern of the cosmos Aether, the illusive 5th element. Spirit element does not follow any particular rule of energy, but rather *is* the rule.

Light workers, medicine people, the enlightened, Lamas of Shambhala and simple earth peoples realize that the Aether acts as a bridge between earth/body and heaven/spirit. A rainbow that embraces all colors, even as spirit embodies all things, makes a suitable representation of this element in sacred space."

Egahi, Shadow Dancer and Two Wolves lifted their eyes above the horizon. Raw energy in the form of a thunder bolt cracked the ceiling of space, in a non-threatening manner. A megastar revealed core center of Anaglisgv with majestic leaders and branches reproducing, pulsating across the galaxy respectfully honoring its source while projecting a luminance of spiraling prisms.

Miko states, "The life force of the Great Mystery is the breath of all of creation. It is so taught in many persuasions that humans are made in the image and likeness of the Creator. Many forget so easily. This labyrinth is but a symbol, a metaphorical roadmap. It is a wise tool. Its purpose is to teach you that *you* are the portal."

Then, drawing a deep breath, she said, "Whatever energy signature we carry will be repeated infinitely, again and again…until we change that vibration. You are fractals of the Great Spirit.

Rick Two Wolves was beginning to understand that he was a warrior of higher purpose. As he had warmly accepted the guidance and companionship of Egahi, Shadow Dancer and Medicine Woman, Miko, he now embraced a new responsibility: unveiling of the light within his own heart spirit to guide and help others. Realizing that they would always be by his side when he needs them, and sometimes when he does not, he would always carry his own wisdom and strengths.

Two Wolves eyed a piece of paper near his foot. It was a bit old and worn, but the words were clearly visible. The wayas circled him and requested he read the message aloud. Dated Mother's Day, 1995; it read:

Dear Mom,

Happy Mother's Day. I want to thank you for everything that you have done for me. I know I said that I was going to get you a gift, but I didn't. I thought this would be better, a homemade card and a little letter of thanks. Thanks for always being there when I am down and happy. Your support and wisdom were always helpful. Even though we have our disagreements, we always worked it out.

Whatever that little light inside of you is, don't let it stop shining. All of us won't know what to do if it did. And I'm pretty sure Michael would agree with me too. All of those little sayings and all the prayers have helped in some way or another. I wish I could say more but my mind is at a blank. I love you mom and I always will.

Happy Mother's Day, Mom.

Love Your Son,
Rick Two Wolves

Dear Mom,

Happy Mother's Day. I want to thank you for everything that you have done for me. I know I said that I was going to get you a gift but I didn't. I thought this would be better. A homemade card and a little letter of thanks. Thanks for always being there when I'm down and happy. Your support and wisdom was always helpful. Even though we have our disagreements, we always worked it out.

Whatever that little light inside of you is, don't let it stop shining. All of us won't know what to do if it did. And I'm pretty sure Michael would agree with me too. All of those little sayings and all the prayers have helped in some way or another. I wish I could say more but my mind is at a blank. I love you mom and I always will.

Happy Mother's Day Mom.

Love, Your son
Rick & Two Rivers

EPILOGUE

From the diary of Calvin:

It wasn't until I turned 30 that I shed that mask and started to feel again. I told myself that my life would be different, and those dark hallways would never haunt me again. Instead, I looked to nature. I stared at trees and marveled at their steadfast existence. They are the rocks of this world, the epitome of strength and survival. I started to take in some of their energy and to make myself stronger. And my life got better. I let go of the past and started to live for today. By the time I was 31, I was happy. I felt steadfast. So, what changed? If I am happy, then why am I taking the time to get all of this out? Well, a couple of months ago, I was given a challenge. One of the doors in one of those dark hallways opened. In that doorway was a person I had long ago locked away. I never expected to have to face her again. It was enough to make me want to yield. I couldn't though. I had to be a man and stand my ground. She has no control over me anymore. She is just a person I used to know. Well, it was then that I realized she does have some control. She *has my name. A name she gave to me when she adopted me, erasing my birth named and the first seven years of my life, Michael Brian Benson. The name of that man that I thought I knew; the man I struggled to become. I was taken back at how powerless I felt. After all of this time, she had the power, or so it seemed. After a few weeks of intense soul searching, I came to a realization. She has no power over me. She does not know the man I fought to become. She does not know the pain I felt, the tears I shed. She knows nothing. She may know the name she gave me, but the person behind that name might as well be invisible to her. And what is a name if the person behind it no longer exists? Words... simple as that. Well, she can have those words. They are not me. I control who I am. So, with my 32nd birthday two days away, I take another step toward becoming me. I let go of the little boy named Brian Michael Davis, whom I no longer remember. I say goodbye to the scared, broken child named Michael Brian Benson. And I become steadfast as the man Calvin Michael. He is all I have ever wanted to be. He is me."*

Calvin Michael

Calvin and Rick

Elizabeth Autry

Elizabeth Davis Autry is a dedicated mom of her daughter, Emelina, and son, William. She is currently a member of the VFW auxiliary of Paragould #2242 and serves as the official Chaplain.

As a former storm chaser she used her knowledge in her work to have a monthly display about what weather and emergency management was needed to prepare in Greene County. She worked with the Director of emergency management and the regional Director that included 5 counties of Northeast Arkansas. She has completed career and leadership classes and has been recognized for her skills and abilities in management. Elizabeth has been a volunteer for the Red Cross.

Rick Two Wolves and Richard Pony Soldier Byrd
at Naming Ceremony

Rick and his Mom, Palmer

Godfrey Benjamin Chipps

Larry Sellers

Chief David Thundering Eagle Fallis

Rick Two Wolves with His Sacred Staff

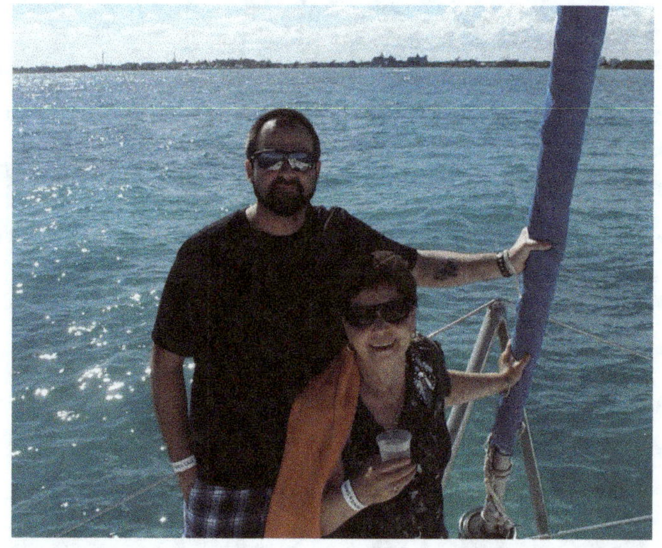

Calvin and his Mom, Donna

FOOTNOTES

Chapter One

1. The Thomas Pecora Show, Broadcast Media Production and Distribution, Chicago, Il. (from Family Reunion, thomaspecora.com/family.html)

2. Horn Chips, American-tribes.com

3. Zitkála-Šáde, Red Bird/Gertrude Simmons Bonnin, https://www.rps.gov—Zitkala-Sa, National Women's History Museum htpps://www.womenshistory.org

Chapter Five

4. Deep Look, PBS Digital Studio, Writer Amy Standen

Chapter Six

5. "Puhpowee" The force that causes mushrooms to push up and appear overnight; (Potawatomi Native American language of the Algonquin family.) The Potawatomi Nation, have a word to describe the force that propels a mushroom out of the ground. "Puhpowee" speaks to the "unseen energies that animate everything." EcoPsychology Initiative. ecopsychologyinitiative.com

6. Fantastic Fungi, a film by Louis Schwartzberg https://www.wired.com

Chapter Seven

7. https://cosmosmagazine.com"Black hole" in popular culture is the ultimate metaphor for an invisible destroyer.

Chapter Fourteen

8. Anihcak is "Kachina" spelled backward. A kachina is a person who represents kachina spirit in ceremonial dances.

Chapter Sixteen

9. Hopi—Messages from the Ancients, Office Tetsu Shiratori https://www.youtube.com/watch?v=Xn-65fJp6m8A

Chapter Eighteen

10. The Sundance https://www.galaudetgallery.com/sundance#:~:text=_TheTwoFeathersMedicine-Clan,withmembersofthissociety.

Chapter Twenty

11. Ahote is the Hopi word for "restless one."

12. https://www.pbs.org/video/hopi-origin-story-dc0awe/

Chapter Twenty-Two

13. https://en.wikipedia.org/wiki/UNESCO

Chapter Twenty-Three

14. Turning into the Earth's Natural Rhythm   https://brainworldmagazine.com/tuning-in-to-the-earths-

natural-rhythm/https://trividafunctionalmedicine. com/the-healing-power-of-sound-the-solfeggio-frequencies/The Solfeggio Frequencies are believed to have been in existence since ancient Hindu cultures first began chanting in Sanskrit. The scale came into popularity during the 10th Century when the Solfeggio Frequencies formed the basis for Gregorian Chants (a form of spiritual music that is a hallmark of the early Roman Catholic Church). In modern times, the scale has been incorporated into all manner of spiritual and "healing" music as well as modern vocal music. In fact, the Solfeggio Frequencies are the basis for the Do-Re-Mi-Fa-So-La-Ti scale. But that's not why the Solfeggio Frequencies matter to health scientists. The Solfeggio's six scales were purported to be associated with specific healing attributes: One can now find "ambient" music and videos tuned to the Solfeggio Frequencies on YouTube and Spotify. Studies have since observed the effects of Gregorian Chants, and other music tuned to the Solfeggio Frequencies, on conditions such as autism, depressed mood, and learning disorders. Other scientific areas of inquiry on the Solfeggio include its effect on the nervous system, the endocrine system, the properties of DNA, and even energetic properties of water. Hospitals have studied the effects of music on how patients heal from surgery. Other studies have examined how music affects people who are in a comatose state and those being treated for serious mental health conditions. Studies have also examined the effects of different types of music on: Athletic performance,work productivity, learning and memory,stress relaxation response, mood and emotion.

14. Power Vs. Force, The Hidden Determinants of Human Behavior by David Hawkins, M.D., PH.D. Hay House, Inc

Chapter Twenty-Five

15. http://www.native-languages.org/legends-dragonfly.htm

ENDNOTES—BIBLIOGRAPHY

Introduction

Joseph Campbell, (born March 26, 1904, New York, U.S.—died October 30, 1987, Honolulu, Hawaii) is a prolific American author and editor whose works on comparative mythology examined the universal functions of myth in various human cultures and mythic figures in a wide range of literatures.

Chapter One

Thomas Pecora, Producer, Host of the Thomas Pecora Show, Chicago. He was an intuitive astrologist who interviewed world known spiritual teachers and authors, including Deepak Chopra.

Miko, Choctaw Medicine Woman, is a fictional character.

Chapter Two

John Muir, Naturalist, writer and advocate of U.S. Forest Conservation, John Muir founded the Sierra Club and helped establish Sequoia and Yosemite National Parks.

Chapter Eight

David James Pelzer is an American author of

several autobiographical and self-help books. His 1995 memoir of childhood abuse, *A child Called "It"* listed on the New York Times Bestseller List for several years, and in five years had sold at least 1.6 million copies.

Chapter Nine

Paige Bartholomew, a licensed psychotherapist, hypnotherapist, intuitive empath, contactee, volunteer soul, and a passionate writer of transformational thought. Paige has been a devoted student of Sufism since 1998, where she is ordained Sufi Master Teacher by the Shadhuliyya Higher Sufi Council.

Chapter Ten

Chief Dan George, OC (born Geswanouth Slahoot; July 24, 1899–September 23, 1981) was a chief of the Tsleil-Waututh Nation, a Coast Salish band whose Indian Reserve is located on Burrard Inlet in the southeast area of the District of North Vancouver, British Columbia, Canada. He also was an actor, musician, poet and an author.

Chapter Eleven

Brian Luke Seaward, Ph.D., author of Stand Like Mountain Flow Like Water, Reflections on Stress and Human Spirituality. Health Communications, Inc. www.hci-online.com

Dr. Elizabeth Armstrong, M.D., American Academy of Medical Acupuncture, Board

Certified in Internal Medicine, Kentucky Board of Medical Licensure. It has been used for thousands of years to promote health, prevent illness and treat various medical problems. Dr. Armstrong brings the unique perspective of a board-certified physician to her practice of acupuncture. She has a special interest in helping oncology patients, stroke patients and those struggling with sports injuries or chronic pain to find relief.https://www.lexingtonmedicalacupuncture.com/about.html

Shen–Tom Williams Ph.D., author of Complete Illustrated Guide to Chinese Medicine, Using Traditional Chinese Medicine for Harmony of Mind and Body. In Traditional Chinese Medicine "it is important to consider that the *Shen* represents the myriad of mental, psychological and also spiritual faculties. It is often said that in Chinese medicine that the health of the *Shen* can be viewed in the eyes."

Rabbi David A. Cooper, author of "God is A Verb and the practice of mystical Judaism" studied mystical Judaism in Jerusalem's Old City for more than eight years and has authored several books on meditation, spiritual retreats and Jewish mystical practices.

Chapter Nineteen

Benjamin Godfrey Chipps, - Lakota from the Oglala Sioux Tribe, a fourth generation Yuwipi Spiritual Interpreter and great grandson of the famed Holy Man Woptura Godfrey Chipps, Sr.—Lakota from the Oglala Sioux Tribe, a fourth generation Yuwipi Spiritual Interpreter and great grandson of the famed Holy Man Woptura.

Transcribed copy of document reference to abuse of children in Arkansas:

CFS 497 Part I Illinois Department of Children
and Family Services
Client Service Plan Narrative

Family Name <u>Benson</u>   Case ID
<u>49689100</u>
Date of Plan <u>09/06/96</u>

Please answer all of the following questions; if this is an initial case plan after children are placed and a current assessment is attached including reasonable efforts check list, skip to Question 5.

What problem(s) brought this case to the attention of the Department? (If child(ren) is in placement, indicate why).

(Past history of abuse and neglect – 2/26/90, Michael and Richard were removed from the Benson's home in Green County, Arkansas, after the children charged the Bensons' with physical abuse – Richard received a head injury that required brief hospitalization, and Michael reported being punched and burned with a cigarette lighter. After a period in foster care, the children were returned home to the Bensons. The Arkansas Child Welfare Services report that following a second abuse charge, the Bensons left the state, taking both boys with them.)
In 1991, Richard reported that his father hit him in the face for not completing his school work. Family First services were put into place; Richard spent 4 weeks in the psychiatric ward of Mercy Hospital.

This case again came to the attention of the Department on 3-17-92 on allegations of abuse and neglect; Richard was found restrained in a car and was admitted to the hospital with a broken toe, broken arm, 3-month old rib fractures, and severely malnourished. Guardianship of both Richard and Michael was given to DCFS on 10/4/93. Criminal charges were filed against the parents on three counts of abuse and neglect. On 6-27-94, the parents were placed on probation for a period of 4 years. Both children remain in foster care.

Summarize significant developments/events in the case since last service plan.

3/4/96 – Robert and Dianna Benson surrendered their parental rights to both Richard and Michael Benson.

ABOUT THE AUTHORS

 **PALMER TOLLY** is a retired Psychotherapist with a Master of Arts Degree in Psychology. She was Board Certified as Professional Counselor by the American Psychotherapy Association.

Her musical achievements as a composer and performer won her an international award from the Native American Music Awards of New York, 2018, for the CD Dreamwalker Suite by People of the Star Orchestra. She is also the Assistant Director of the Metropolitan Contemporary Jazz Orchestra. She constantly strives to bring an awareness of humanity through her creativity of music and literature, which also includes her publication of *Chronicles of Two Wolves: A Path to Heart Spirit* through Rabbit House Press.

In her twenty years as a Licensed Clinical Professional counselor in Illinois, Palmer presented workshops at universities and colleges on various topics of wellness in the Chicago region. Often joined by Chief Joseph Big Feather Schallmo, of the Two Feathers Medicine Clan, they imparted knowledge from both the traditional and the Indigenous modalities for healing heart and spirit. Palmer gained a reputation for being an effective psychotherapist in the areas of anxiety disorders, including Post Traumatic Stress, Depression and

Eating Disorders. She was contracted by the Illinois Dept. of Family and Children Services to work with children and adult victims of abuse.

Palmer created, produced and presented a symposium entitled "Caring for the Mind, Body & Spirit, (An Enlightened Perspective on Wellness). This one-day conference gave a forum to teachers in fields that included: Acupuncture, Psychotherapy, Native American wisdom and complimentary treatment options by medical professionals.

In pursuit of her quest for spiritual knowledge, Palmer traveled to New York to attend Lessons given by the Dalai Lama. An insatiable yearning to humbly share the company of adepts was fulfilled through many endearing relationships with Indigenous peoples from the Chicago/Indiana area. Members of the Two Feathers Medicine Clad requested to build a Sweat Lodge *(Inipi)* on her property on the Kankakee River. Medicine People were frequent guests as well.

It is the intention of this author to convey authenticity and originality for hope, illumination and miracles. Palmer offers it as a shout out to the universe, that in spite of whatever has been done to you—you are a vessel of light.

JAMES RIORDAN

Rare is it that any author will have one of his books described as the *definitive* work on a particular subject, but such a distinction has been bestowed by critics on no less than four books written by James Riordan. The New York Times Bestseller *Break on Through*, Riordan's biography of Doors lead singer Jim Morrison, has not only been called *"the most objective, thorough and professional Morrison biography"* by the *Times Book Review* but also named as one of the *Ten All Time Best Rock Biographies* by Amazon.com. Riordan's *The Platinum Rainbow* (written with Bob Monaco) was called *"One of the best how-to books ever written"* by the *Los Angeles Daily News* and *"The ultimate career book on the music industry"* by *Recording, Engineer & Producer*. Critics described Riordan's *The Bishop of Rwanda* as *"one of the most important books you'll ever read."* and *The Coming of the Walrus*, Riordan's novel about the 60's as *"the definitive book on the era"* and *"a hilarious tale of a harrowing search for the greatest truth of all"*. With the release of *A Well Thought Out Scream* and *Madman in the Gate*, Riordan pushed the boundaries again with poetry/song lyric books that contain hundreds of stunning, beautiful and poignant images from artists and photographers from all over the world.

The author of forty books, James Riordan's career began in the music industry whereas a songwriter, manager, producer and concert promoter he worked with several well known artists. In 1976, he began writing a newspaper column on popular music, *Rock-Pop*, which he later syndicated. Riordan soon became one of America's premier rock journalists with articles reaching millions of readers including those of *Rolling Stone, Crawdaddy, Circus, Musician,* and newspapers like *The Chicago Daily News, The Kansas City Star,* and many others. His reputation for relating on a one-to-one level soon led to interviews with George Harrison, Bob Dylan, Fleetwood Mac, Frank Zappa, The Doobie Brothers, Kenny Rogers, Barbara Mandrell, Crosby, Stills &Nash and countless others (written with Bob Monaco in 1980) became the largest selling book ever written about the music business. The guide to "succeeding in the music business without selling your soul" was praised by *Variety,The Chicago Tribune, The Los Angeles Times, The Las Vegas Sun, The Minneapolis Tribune, Billboard, Record World* and many more. *The Platinum Rainbow* became an industry wide phenomenon and interviews with James Riordan were aired on over 1200 radio stations and numerous television talk shows. Next Riordan collaborated with Pulitzer Prize winner Jason Miller on a mini-series for network television *The Irish* and a movie of the week for CBS *Bless Me Father*.

In June 1991, William Morrow published *Break on Through* to outstanding sales and reviews. Riordan was a consultant on Oliver Stone's film of Morrison's life, *The Doors*, which led to his writing Stone's biography. Published by Hyperion in December

1995, *Entertainment Weekly* called *STONE* "an unflinching biography...enough spectacle to fill a month of daytime–TV talk shows." *The New York Post* said reading the book was like *"the sensory overload of watching all of Oliver Stone's movies back-to-back."* Riordan was interviewed by *Inside Edition, People Magazine, Tom Snyder,* and many others. From 1997-2000, Riordan created and co-starred in a local TV program, *Kankakee Valley Prime Time,* which won six Crystal Communicators, three Tellys, and earned Riordan a Chicago/Midwest Emmy Nomination for Writing. In the summer of 1999, James Riordan wrote, directed and starred in *Maddance,* an hour-long dramatic project which won Crystal Communicators for Drama, Writing, Acting and Directing. He has written several screenplays since including *John Horse* which won Best Screenplay at the San Antonio Film Festival in 2018.